CHOCOLATE CAKE
FOR IMAGINARY LIVES

Genevieve Jenner

First published in 2022 by Deixis Press
www.deixis.press
ISBN 978-1-8384987-2-6

Cover design by Libby Alderman
paperyfeelings.co.uk

Typeset using Sabon

ℭ

CHOCOLATE CAKE
FOR IMAGINARY LIVES

Genevieve Jenner

Deixis Press

To Onion and Biscuit,
the two most entertaining people I have ever met.

C

RECIPES

𝒞

DEAD DOVE

Yesterday at work someone put a paper bag labelled *dead dove I do not eat* in the fridge. Now I want to find them and ask them to marry me. Anyone can write a passive-aggressive note to not eat their yogurt or Cobb salad, but this was almost a dare. I had never eaten dove. I had drinks with someone once who went on at length about Tierra de Campos being the place to have squab. I refused to go beyond that one drink, so I never knew if they were correct. I wondered if it was a regular dead dove that required the services of the work fridge as an ad-hoc morgue. A freezer might have made more sense for that sort of thing. When I was a child my best friend's parents were a vet and a biologist. This meant the occasional run-in with dead animals in the freezer in our pursuit of an ice lolly. My favourite find was the goldfinch that had lace-like ice crystals on its yellow feathers, placed so casually next to a bag of peas.

I opened the fridge again and looked at the bag. How does one prepare dove for lunch? Was it part of a leftover pie? Considering how lazy I am about laundry, my chances seemed worth the risk of having my nose pecked off. When Colin from marketing and his salad of quinoa saturated with a cheerless dressing of self-satisfied aspirations had finally left, I opened the bag. It was a pigeon—with a face! (It looked mildly bemused, as if I had interrupted its nap.) It looked like the ducks that hang in the windows of Chinatown restaurants, but much smaller. It looked so beautiful and glossy. There wasn't much flesh, just enough for someone's lunch—in a selfish, perverse moment I decided: *my* lunch. It was luscious. Like a surprising kiss that continues a little longer than anticipated. Though it had been in the fridge, the skin was crispy and slightly sweet. I could taste ginger, garlic and something like vinegar but much richer. In the bag there was also a small container with a couple of lemon slices. I squeezed it onto the meat and it lifted everything even more, making me feel flushed and excited. I began to wonder if I could cook this. How to get the recipe without giving myself away? I finished the bird, disposed of the bones, and then placed my sad sandwich inside the bag (I wasn't a complete bastard. I would never leave anyone hungry) and placed it back into the fridge. I quickly scribbled a note asking *How do I make that pigeon?* and slipped the piece of paper into the bag, then left.

Tuesday. I had limp pasta, and curiosity over what I might find in the fridge. The bag was still there—as was the now day-old tuna sandwich. And a note.

You must provide me with something better if you wish to know how to make that dish. Sandwiches and salad don't cut it.

Today I would have to eat my little lunch and find a way to please this chef. I didn't know where to find a pigeon with ease. Were they looking for entremets? A complete peacock redressed in its feathers? I would present them with my own subtlety. It wouldn't be four and twenty blackbirds baked into a pie, but I knew it would have many flavours. After work I gathered ingredients from the supermarket. Yes, I even spent the money on pistachios, as I was preparing a dish for an honoured guest. Whoever they are.

I ate cheese on toast for supper and began to sauté pieces of chicken. No puritan chicken breasts that try to flirt with gilded decadence in the high church of seasoning. Thighs and legs were needed. Something that has an unashamed relationship with flavour and adapts quickly to assorted culinary desires. I set them aside while cooking down onions and garlic in spices that spread their perfume in the most generous way—like an auntie's expensive scent that lingers on babies and children after many hugs. Warmth and cosiness. I had to add more cinnamon. And saffron. This dish needed a little more life. Between stock, eggs, nuts, and everything else, a pastilla was born in between the delicate sheets of phyllo and butter. I dusted it with sugar at the end so that the meal would begin with a mystery: "Is it sweet? Is it savoury?"

The following day, I placed two slices in a container in the dove bag as an offering. (Always two slices. In my eyes it is a sin to leave anyone unsatiated.) I wanted to watch like one waiting for elves to make shoes, but there were meetings and other inane tasks to trudge through. When I returned later, I opened the fridge and bag to a container empty of pastilla. It had been cleaned, and within it resided the recipe for Chinese fried pigeon, with the comments: *A specialty in Hong Kong. Your contribution was worthy. Leave me your recipe and I might allow you to be greedy another day.* I took my prize and left my own, with an added note: *The best dishes and gifts require a little wrapping.*

How long would I have to wait before something would appear? Would my recipe be rewarded? I hedged my bets and brought hummus and vegetables, and a slightly woody satsuma. (It is what I call my "pretend diet lunch", as it will always be followed by a furtive, stress-induced Snickers around 3pm when the lunch proves to be unsatisfying.)

It appeared when I was about to give in and pick something out of spite from the vending machine. A note on top of the goods. *You asked for something to undo. Your pastilla nearly undid me. Don't forget the salsa.* Tamales! Parcels, wrapped with care using corn husks. I untied one and tasted the fluffy and moist masa that hid the filling of poblano chillies and cheese. There wasn't the usual watery jarred sauce calling itself salsa. This was salsa verde. Slightly sweeter because the tomatillos had been roasted. I might have been happy just tasting that, but I remembered to add it to the tamales. This person wanted to cause me to lose my emotional balance. They had wiped my memory of what I had eaten at noon. Something with vegetables? This was my lunch and saviour now.

There had been three tamales; I briefly thought I might save one for later, but one shouldn't lie to oneself about food. It was eaten. Quickly. No recipe though. I would have to earn it with another dish. I had no idea where I was being guided, but I knew I wanted to please. I would leap across the Mediterranean this time and produce something that brought out passionate arguments about how it ought to be made.

Gazpacho. It isn't just a few vegetables, old bread, and some tomatoes blended together and served cold. From village to village it can shift in appearance. Most don't realize it can come in a number of colours, and some people insist upon certain ingredients. I wouldn't have a búcaro to serve it in, but I would make sure they knew they were having something different. I began with the most sensual, life-giving force in the garden: garlic. Mashed down with a pestle so it can release that sticky, unashamed scent. I had gone to the bakery at the end of the day to buy a baguette that had been waiting for me. It was stale enough. I tore it apart and let it soak in water before adding it to the waiting garlic. People think tomatoes are the base to gazpacho, but they are not. The bread and garlic—the foundation of comfort and pleasure—will do things to the vegetables (and hopefully my teasing chef) that will touch them with life. Salt, olive oil and vinegar are a clever trio of muses who enhance existence. Tempting the tongue with the possibilities of going this way and that, but still allowing one to keep one's balance. What I made was so inexact. Breaking down a bit of this and that and slowly turning it into a puree that was much more than its appearance might suggest. It wasn't just a soup. It was a meditative elixir.

I waited the next day to put it in the fridge (along with loose instructions on how to make it, and a small container of garnish. Details mattered between us now) because the soup should be chilled but not iced. Then I ran off to file reports and pretend I knew what I was saying when I threw around empty phrases to fill the space and time that makes up work. I wanted that recipe, and to have my taste buds astonished.

At the end of the day, again there was a clean container with the paper token and a further note. *You weren't honest with your recipe. There must have been something else in there. What was it? Are we going to add secret ingredients now?*

This game had taken a different path in the woods. Where would we end up? The next day my senses were thrown into an ocean. *Mul naengmyeon* would force me to relearn every sense. A new cold soup. A pheasant-based broth (the note told me to look out for certain things as if I was on a scavenger hunt, but it gave me a few clues) with long buckwheat noodles that I had to slurp—being dainty was for others, not for anyone eating this. It took me a while to eat it. I had to stare at the arrangement of the noodles, vegetables, pickled radish, the mustard oil floating on the surface, the seeds offering more texture, and the boiled egg. Scattered layers that had such an exact placement. This artist knew what they had to say. It was an abstract painting in a bowl. What were they trying to tell me? I almost felt angry by the end. I had felt too much in public and I had no way of stopping my feelings. I was powerless. In that sudden rage and excitement, I wanted to seek a kind of revenge and make them taste something that was almost too much. Maybe offer them an ortolan and a towel and a note saying: *Top that. Use the towel twice. Once to cover your head and once to wipe your tears.* That would be seen as a tantrum. Instead I would find a way to drown them on land.

I claimed I had a dentist appointment. Instead I woke up early and bought octopus from the market. They even cleaned it and removed the beak for me. I came home with that, prawns, and a citron. My spite was leading me towards many suppers of cheese on toast that week. In my kitchen I massaged the octopus and quickly boiled it. (My *nonnina* said massaging it would make it tender and gentle. She thought it needed to be treated well one last time before offering itself. She found spirits in everything. She also cooked hers with a wine cork. My wine was cheap and screw-top.) I found myself at 9am on my tiny balcony barbecuing octopus and prawns. If the neighbours said anything, I would bring up how I said nothing about those parties where their guests left vomit or knickers on my doorstep. (Always have a means of blackmailing neighbours who think they are DJs.) Setting aside the seafood, I grilled artichoke hearts. Smoke would touch nearly everything, its own elusive perfume. Then it was a race. Soon it would be lunch and I had to make this imaginary appointment end in time. Chopping up the octopus, tossing it together with the prawns and artichokes, dressing it quickly with olive oil, small pieces of citron (and a touch of the juice), the feathery leaves of fennel found in the park, celery leaves, capers, and that loving sprinkle of salt. Nothing else. They should taste like a moment by the beach on a warm day. Where lunches are lazy and intimate.

I made it to work, slipped it into the bag that held secrets, and made a bit of a show to my manager about being threatened with a root canal. The truly great performances are not on screen but in lies told to bosses where medical issues allegedly exist. I was impatient. Sleep deprivation and excitement are almost as good as inebriation but terrible to experience at work. By the afternoon search for coffee, I had to check the fridge. There was a note that said, *Are you a witch? You have stolen something from me today with that dish. I will find a way to retrieve it. Tomorrow I leave you a simple treasure.*

I went home early. I was craving sleep, though I was worried it wouldn't come that night. I kept considering dishes. Wondering if I could ever match them. Would my imagination fail me? Would my appetite to please ruin me? My ambition could turn into something reckless and obsessive. Morning came once more, and lunch brought me a sandwich. Was this a violation of the rules? Or were they allowed to do as they please? It came with a note:

I had this sandwich once. Long ago. On a street. Sitting on a curb where loitering was an encouraged past-time. Let this sandwich haunt you. P.S. don't forget to look under the cup by the microwave.

This wasn't a challenge. This was someone showing me their heart. This wasn't just any bread. It was *pane di Altamura*. The kind of bread that sings when you break it. It was filled with fresh chevre, prosciutto, and fig jam. A few simple fillings that stand prettily on their own, but together they become like Schubert's Piano Trio No. 2. I was being led with authority to experience a taste of their own longing to go back to that street. Every flavour was available to us. We didn't need to be anywhere else.

Once I finished I wanted to return to the beginning. I looked at the note again: the cup. Under that cup was a perfectly ripe persimmon. And another note: *Eat me with a spoon.* Would I grow big or small? I cut it in half and began to eat this honey sweet pudding that made me briefly wonder if I was hallucinating because I thought I could taste cinnamon. I returned to the surroundings when Colin and his acai bowl wanted to get to the utensils. I couldn't stay in that room and listen to him discuss chia seeds. I had to hide away because I felt that persimmon on my lips, my tongue, and every other nerve ending. I needed more. I had to capture that moment. There was only one way to do that. Yes, there would be food, but sometimes one leaps out of the kitchen because there is more to be done. I was without sleep again.

I arrived the next day in my altered state to a tragedy.

Our bag was gone. Someone had cleaned out the fridge (leaving a shaming note about people not being considerate of others). I had two creations. Where would our secrets reside now? One could not be hidden under a cup. It was time for a declaration that was taped to the fridge:

Persimmons are only for people who understand ephemeral joy
The ones who appreciate the cordial torture of anticipation
Dear khormaloo, that fruit of the Gods, likes to play coy
That brilliant titian with its pert nose doesn't offer easy elation
It demands to be put on display so that you can watch it ripen
Eventually those days of waiting (with quick touches) come to pass
Cupping that soft candy-sweetness, all senses seem to heighten
Yet that ambrosial toothsome flesh is gone too fast. Alas.

Though the fridge was clean, and the cups were washed and put away, the cupboard remained full of forgotten bags. I took one, and wrote, *Loaves and Fishes: more where that came from,* and placed a salmon and dill piroshky in it. I put it in the fridge for someone's lunch.

C

CHOCOLATE CAKE
FOR IMAGINARY LIVES

We all have imaginary lives, and if we are lucky we have a dish to go with them.

You begin by making a cup of strong coffee. I tend to use espresso. I think of that scene in "The Freshman" where espresso is made and lots of sugar is added, and it is implied that drinking it will make you a man. Really it just makes you feel like you are on a speed trip. Maybe this is what the Italians are aiming for? They get up, have that tiny dose of coffee and then race around in their cars, engaging in scandal. Then they cause the government to fall, all before lunch. This is also why every place closes for a few hours in the afternoon. Everyone needs to recover as they begin to come down from the morning espresso/scandal frenzy. Then they spend the afternoon reading about the morning scandal. If that isn't enough, they engage in their own private scandal (that long-standing affair with the spouse of an old family friend), and maybe go for a walk to clear their head before dinner. Unfortunately, you won't be doing that with your coffee. Though you could, but you would need to make a second cup of coffee that would need to cool—if you still want to make this cake.

Cream together four ounces of softened butter (and for all that is holy don't try and use cold butter, or speed up the process by using a microwave it to soften it. Get the butter out when you are making the coffee. While you wait for things to cool down or warm up, you can read about pleasant scandals while drinking that cup of coffee. See, there is a rhythm to all of this.) with eight ounces of granulated sugar and seven and a half ounces of brown sugar. If there are small people lurking about, you may have to keep them from taking tastes of the butter and sugar. Add two eggs (one at a time) and beat until smooth. In another bowl (because we are going to dirty many dishes today. Just accept this now.) you will whisk together one half cup of cocoa powder with one half cup of boiling water. What you want to achieve here is a smooth paste (like you would if you were making hot chocolate from scratch). Pour that into your butter/sugar/egg mixture and mix until things are dark and chocolatey. Sift in eight ounces of flour and one teaspoon of baking soda. You want to mix this just enough so that there aren't any white streaks left.

Then you can return to your coffee that has been sitting on the counter looking woeful. Pour that into the thick cake batter along with one half teaspoon of vanilla. Mix mix mix, and it will turn into a fairly thin batter. But that will be alright. You will pour the batter into two 8- or 9-inch pans (which will have been greased and floured and, if you are one for details, lined with parchment) and bake at 350°F/180°C for about 20 or 25 minutes. As with most cakes, you will want to do the toothpick test to make sure it is done. This isn't some molten lava cake, folks. We aren't going to burn our tongues and then slightly regret dessert. Take the cake out and let it cool on racks before you think about frosting anything.

As you wait you can read some Dante and reflect upon how that Florentine understood humanity and all its foibles and did it so beautifully in the common tongue. Or you can slouch to one side in a slip dress, wearing dark glasses, and pretend you are in a Fellini film. You are on your own for finding circus freaks and sex workers to stand around with you. God, this coffee is good.

Now it is time to assemble your cake. For the filling you could put in raspberry jam or apricot jam (if you want to pay a sort of homage to Sachertortes but don't want to wrestle with trying to get a mirror-perfect chocolate icing.) I had chocolate raspberry jam in the cupboard. If you really want chocolate raspberry jam but only have the raspberry, why not melt down an ounce of unsweetened chocolate and mix it in with some jam? Ta-da. Spread about a third of a cup on the bottom layer of your cake. Then pop the other layer on top.

Then we come to the question of icing. We want to avoid something grainy and disappointing that puts the brakes on the passionate momentum that is building with this cake. Melt down a few ounces of sweetened chocolate (anywhere between four and six will suffice) in a pan over simmering water. Take that off the heat and add about one half cup of sour cream. Not light sour cream, thank you. We are having cake, not penance. Maybe add one half teaspoon of vanilla if you are up for it. Or maybe some bourbon. Yes. Bourbon. Once you have whisked everything together and it is a silky satin brown, you will want to spread that all over the cake. (It should be just this side of warm). Do a crumb layer of icing, and then spread the rest over the cake. It will look lovely.

The wonderful thing about this cake is the variety of flavours and textures. The cake itself is moist and very sweet, and there is the tartness of the raspberry filling and the balance of sweet and sour from the soft frosting. The flavour is a little more sophisticated. Not that there's anything wrong with the likes of confetti cake and red velvet, but this is a cake for adults with petty problems and a desire to flirt with chaos and embrace a little madness.

This is a cake where you recall a heady weekend in someone's *Schloss* (especially if you use apricot jam) sometime between the wars. You were only going as the guest of a friend of a friend, but you stayed far longer than you thought, because you became acquainted with a gentleman. He had rumours swirling about him being some Russian duke who had to leave his country, and of being a cad who was likely the bastard child of some minor noble from a backwater in Swabia. You didn't really care because the cake was good and he was charming. It was likely having that cake with him on a picnic that sealed the deal to become his mistress.

Of course, you could only stay for a while because life got in the way and you had to return to work in the bookshop. Like Fellini said, "There is no beginning. There is no end. There is only the passion of life." Have some in your cake.

ℰ

FLIP FOR THE SOUTHERN GOTHIC

When well-ossified on corn liquor, my father would say of my mama's ancestors, "If you have to leave Louisiana because of scandal, even the devil tips his hat in respect." When they married, my father took Mama away from Georgia up to Maryland, in case the family insanity was catching, like measles or ringworm.

When we were obliged to make a Christmas pilgrimage out of built-up guilt, I would be given a severe haircut and told to mumble amen to prayers I was supposed to know.

Mama's family was filled with the most desperate and devout people who clutched their rosary beads the way a dope fiend might hold a spoon. There were three acceptable activities in the family house: offering up novenas, alluding to someone's dark secrets, and drinking. The latter two went together, as novenas didn't offer much opportunity for conversation unless you were talking to God—and like my departed granddaddy, God didn't say much.

My father would spend much of the visit standing in front of the house smoking, looking like a tired lawn ornament. Except when flips were being made. It was a drink that would bring everyone into the house. Even that one distant cousin (who mostly slept in the barn because she said she smelled sin upon people) would make an appearance.

They had to use a hot poker to make this libation because Grandmère was convinced that the stove was secretly a Baptist, as it broke every time she tried to cook with booze. She conceded defeat the day she tried to make figgy pudding and the oven door fell off.

Cousin Thibodeaux (who lived in the rickety shed that Grandmère called the summer house) was put in charge of mixing together rum and molasses in a large pitcher. He remarked as he poured in another healthy measure of rum, "One year, a certain relation tried to mark themselves with that poker, after dealings with that passing Father from Valdosta."

Mama's third sister Lisette—a woman who had been sent home from the convent because she was deemed too excitable—slammed the bowl of eggs on the table. She whispered, "Thibodeaux, that priest was tan from his years as a missionary. I will not have you suggest things before the child."

Thibodeaux, staring at the poker in the fire, muttered, "Cousin, crack me some of those eggs. As you seem to understand cracking up all too well."

Auntie Lisette cracked several eggs into the rum, and molasses, and called out to Mama, "Sister-Child, do you have the beer?" Mama came up from the cellar with her first sister Fanchon, both carrying large pitchers of beer. Fanchon was Mama's eldest sister, a shy older woman who sent me books and hand-knitted socks for my birthday.

I asked Mama, "Why does everyone call you Sister-Child?" Fanchon answered as she poured the beer into the rum and molasses, "Because she was not quite mine, but—"

Grandmère interrupted, "Fanchon, hush now with your nonsense. Is everything ready?" She stuck the hot poker into the pitcher and stirred the foaming liquid, which smelled like burned sugar and warm earth. Once everything was warm, Grandmère put the poker back by the fire. Mama and Auntie Fanchon poured the contents back and forth between the two pitchers before pouring the flips into ceramic tumblers. Thibodeaux sprinkled a bit of nutmeg over the foam, and the adults drank up. As I was now twelve, Fanchon offered me a tiny glass. It was like swallowing spice-scented mud, but then my face and stomach felt warm and numb, which was a distinctly pleasant sensation to experience at ten in the morning.

After having a few drinks, Fanchon began to pet my hair. She said, "Hair just like his granddaddy's." Which struck me as odd. I said, "Auntie Fanchon, I thought Granddaddy's hair was dark. Mine's red. Like Mama's."

Thibodeaux said, "And just like that Yankee who fell off the widow's walk and broke his neck at Fanchon's Cotillion."

Thibodeaux might as well have dropped poison into everyone's drinks, because the immediate hysteria was unlike anything else. When Fanchon was sick on an antimacassar that hadn't been moved since reconstruction, my father led me by the shoulder out to the porch, and said, "Let's go for a drive before that poker gets thrown about again."

ℰ

MACARONI AND CHEESE:
A MEDITATION

You are reading a magazine while waiting for that tyre to be fixed (again), and you see a recipe for a fun way to jazz up that weeknight supper of macaroni and cheese. (We shall not speak of those crime scenes involving zucchini, or peas.) You pause and think of the last time you attempted to add some extra aged gouda and a little garlic to the macaroni and cheese, and how certain members of the dining table objected and spent much of the meal offering as much criticism as Gore Vidal on Norman Mailer. (At least those offended members of the table are adorable and won't go on television programs to deride your dinner-making skills.) How does one satisfy the urge to make dinner a little more interesting and satisfy the desires of the table to eat the same exact thing every single time?

Like recipes for macaroni and cheese, there are a few philosophical approaches to handling this exhausting journey of nightly dinner-making. My mother, a faithful Catholic (who has a soft spot for the Jesuits) was inclined towards a succinct response to any complaints: "Offer it up for Christ's sake."

There are times when one can turn to Camus on those tiring Tuesday nights and say to oneself, "The struggle itself is enough to fill a man's heart. One must imagine Sisyphus happy." When your partner or children ask what you are mumbling about, you say, "Just enjoying the absurdity of existence. Please pick up your socks before I lose my mind."

There is another way that combines multiple philosophical views. You must make dinner and submit to the ritual, but you aren't being punished for trying to pull one over on the Gods. This is a path you are on, and your dining companions are with you—but they must be made aware of the path.

Let's begin by boiling some salted water. You will drop the macaroni in there (and we understand that sometimes in life we must make do with whatever pasta we have on hand. Pasta forgives and knows that life is not a rehearsal.) While the pasta does what it needs to do, we shall make a roux for the cheese sauce. It will be the foundation to possible joy. You will warm about 500ml of milk. On occasion we must bow to the rules of life, and that means no skim milk. In a saucepan you will melt down a bit of butter over medium heat. The British might say a knob of butter, some might say a couple of tablespoons. If we allowed the Danish opinion, they might say, "Enough to spread on a piece of bread and allow tooth marks to be made when you bite into it." (The Danish are good at taking delight in little things, as they live in a culture where things must be kept inside for the sake of the group. Politely dysfunctional we call that, but let's leave the Danish to their sandwiches.)

You will whisk in a third of a cup of flour (30ish grams if you aren't American) and you want things to be light, without lumps, and you must pay attention (you don't want it brown). Someone may come in and ask what is for dinner, and you will say "macaroni and cheese," and they will say, "How are you going to make it? You aren't going to add Red Leicester again, are you? Because it made it weird." You look up and smile. You might say to your children, "It is time to learn non-attachment if you want to truly understand joy. And not just the joy you get when you are allowed to eat as much Easter Candy as you want and hang about in your pajamas half the day playing Roblox until your eyes go a bit crinkly."

They will sigh and say, "Can I have a snack? I am soooooo hungry." You realize the roux MIGHT be close to being a disaster and say, "Fine, whatever, but NO MORE COOKIES. We are eating soon," and you add the milk a bit at a time, whisking a lot and thinking to yourself that maybe Sisyphus applies more to the laundry than to cooking, because at least there is variety with dinner. Though maybe pushing the rock brought new experiences every day. Maybe he saw a small iridescent beetle scurrying by, or there was a point in his day where there was a vista he appreciated. Was that where his happiness might have come from?

Whisk and let the roux slowly thicken. Now you have a choice. You can be English and add a little mace. A bit of depth but nothing showy. Or you can toss in a bit of nutmeg like the Italians. The nutmeg has opinions and will join the dance well. Next you will add some grated cheese. This is your place to cause chaos. Yes, the audience may desire the reliable mix of sharp and medium cheddar. But don't give in easily. Capitulation will not teach them joy. Not yet. Find a combination of strong flavours. Maybe some chevre, gouda, some sort of nutty cheese from Switzerland or France that melts well, a cheese with some jalapeño, a really sharp cheddar that makes your jaw ache, a Double Gloucester with chives? BE the creator! (About three cups of grated cheese will do what you need.) Stir everything; let the cheese surrender to the warmth of the roux. An orgy of flavour from which it will never recover. Let the cheese sauce, and a few people, be undone by this impermanent reality.

Take a moment to check on the macaroni. This is one of the few times you don't want it al dente. See? There are no sure things, even with pasta. You do want the macaroni fairly well done. (If it appears done, drain, save a bit of the pasta water and let it wait a moment.) Quick, back to the sauce: add a quarter cup of beer. Nothing dark and complicated like a moody Irish writer with two common-law wives, living in a falling down mansion that is slowly being eaten by wisteria. You want a nice light ale. A friendly sort of beer that won't cause problems and will leave you saying, "Yeah, that's all right." Keep stirring. The cheese should

19

be melted; add a bit of salt and pepper for flavour, and if you feel like doing something mad like adding in paprika to terrify your diners because it appears awfully orange, you do that. Bring surprises to the table. We must understand how transient our surroundings are.

Now to combine the pasta and cheese sauce. Maybe add a bit of that pasta water if things need it. You know your cheese sauce, you know your reality, even though it shifts and changes like the shoreline every single day. Put everything in an oven-safe dish. We must experience a little ephemeral decoration. Like going on a walk and spotting a rogue mushroom growing on an old post, or the curl of wild roses around an old tree, it is good when the creator places unplanned beauty before us. With macaroni and cheese, you can add some panko crumbs on top, extra cheese, maybe some finely chopped bacon, crispy fried onions, or tiny sliced cherry tomatoes. Let there be texture and another flavour. The creator terrifies and delights.

Place the macaroni and cheese in the oven at 350°F/180°C for about 15–20 minutes. Remove it once it is done; admire it and serve it up. Should anyone complain that it isn't the usual thing, take a sip of your drink and say, "Why cling to the macaroni and cheese that was? Embrace the macaroni and cheese you have before you, children. Appreciate wonder when it arrives in your world. When you accept the macaroni and cheese as it is in your journey, you may experience a hint of the Tao. And eat your damn vegetables."

DEARER THAN FREEDOM

We expected tomatoes in July. We did not expect the sky to rain upon us with fire.

By September, the English and American comrades were being called home. There were few tomatoes. Dunixi would always insist that the *sopa* needed tomatoes, and eggs. He came from a village where his mother and aunties put tomatoes into the *sopa*.

It was decided among the remaining few that we should walk towards the border. The news was not good there, but it was worse elsewhere. Everything had been abandoned or burned. The Fascists ruled the cemetery that was once Donostia.

A day from the border, we found a *choza* to sleep in. A shepherd with a weather-battered beret arrived to find us gleaning garlic and small wrinkled tomatoes from the dying garden. Dunixi smiled at me and said, "*Sopa!*" Dunixi had been born on a feast day. He lived every day like it.

The shepherd did not object to our presence. He offered his olive oil to eat our bread. I told him that he must save it for another day. The shepherd held up the jug and said, "I am old. I do not have the time to wait for a better day."

I felt around my pockets for one of the few remaining cigarettes given to me by the crazy Hungarian with the camera. I offered one to the shepherd. A small payment for the oil. He accepted it. He crouched near the small fire and lit it. He kept his gun and dog close.

Dunixi said, "Miren, where is the paprika? You must make the *sopa*!" I reminded him that we were saving it for when we crossed the border. He dismissed me with a wave of his hand. He turned to our comrades, and said, "We can have Miren's *sopa de ajo*! It solves every bit of weariness. Her soup would have brought Christ back in two days instead of three."

He said to the shepherd, "*Lagun* [friend], do you have a pot?" The old man pointed to the one near the choza. I poured the oil into the pot and let it warm over the fire. I minced the cloves of garlic and sliced up the stale bread. I tossed the garlic and a spoonful of paprika into the pot. It crackled with the same rhythm as a flamenco dancer. The dance settled down when I placed the slices of bread into the pot. Turned them over to soften in the hot oil. I called to someone to bring me a jug of water. One of the comrades handed me the jug and said, "If Dunixi has some *sopa*, I hope he will speak of something else. It is all I have heard of from him for days." The water was poured over the bread. I stirred and waited for things to come to a boil. Then a little salt. As I stirred and broke down the bread, the *sopa* slowly turned into a savoury porridge. I poured a splash of wine into the pot. It was more like vinegar. It had been carried for weeks in the heat. It would do. Dunixi, who was speaking to the other comrades, called out, "The *sopa* is blessed, and so shall be all who taste it. Where are the tomatoes, Miren?"

"You can have your Auntie's *sopa* another day."

"Miren, where are the eggs to stir in at the end? The eggs make it magic."

"Do you see any hens about? Are you wrong in the head?"

He smiled and poked about in his knapsack. He stood up. He was a magician conjuring two eggs. He held them up and called out, "Eggs for my darling Miren!"

A crack came through the trees. Dunixi stumbled to the ground along with the eggs. The yolks mixed with his blood. He was gone without having tasted his beloved *sopa*.

I cried out, "*Nire maitasuna!*" My love!

Those were the last words of Basque I ever spoke aloud. That language died with Dunixi. I never made *sopa de ajo* again for men, either. Only women. For they don't mind the taste of sorrow within the soup—a flavour they taste every single day of their lives.

WHEN YOU WANT THAT

Sometimes I like to think about the Great Canadian Maple Syrup Heist. They were out to make money. I would have just hoarded the syrup and imbibed it like some kind of degenerate. Thankfully life hasn't come to that point. But there have been close moments. To stay on the right side of civility while still getting my fix, I like to make maple cream pie. It is for those of us who need near instant gratification in pie form. We know who we are. (Meetings are Tuesday at the first Baptist church at 7pm. The coffee is okay, and sometimes someone brings doughnuts. Maple bars, natch.)

To make this saucy little delight you need a pre-baked pie-shell. Sometimes you are a monastic sort who derives pleasure out of pouring your little heart and soul into making pastry. Enjoying the ritual of rolling out the dough, forming it in the pie pan, and baking it. Then of course cooling and waiting. Maybe do a few decades of the rosary while you wait. Or you can just buy one from the grocery store because you are getting the itches. Now let's make that filling. Get out your saucepan and pour in a cup and a half of maple syrup. Yes, that is a lot, but many things are A LOT in life and we still keep going. Listening to that relation talk about how much they paid for some property is A LOT. Sitting on a train next to that person who keeps sniffing loudly is A LOT.

At least this will make you happy and you won't roll your eyes … too much.

Then add a cup of heavy or double cream. Warm that up over medium heat. In a little bowl, whisk together a quarter cup of corn flour or starch and a quarter cup of water. It should be smooth. Slowly whisk that into your maple cream. Continue whisking and bring it to a low boil. You don't want to scorch anything. It should thicken. Then pour it into your pie shell. Put it in the fridge for a bit. While you wait for it to set up you can pour some maple syrup into your coffee. Don't look at me like that. It isn't half bad. I am not judging you. I mean … yes, I *am* judging you, but for other things, and I keep that to myself.

Once it is all chilled and pretty you have a slice. Or three. Feel mildly unwell but deny it to everyone. Sure, you went too far, but that is your choice. Then wait an hour and have another slice. Maybe a nap too. It is the holidays; we do what we want.

☙

KIKI'S TIKI
AND OTHER PLACES WE LAMENT

Kiki's Tiki wasn't too good to live; it was a comet that some were lucky to experience. People who were there will occasionally pause and say, "Remember when Miss Gigi would perform in the lounge with her Sérgio Mendes tribute act?" or, "And that pu-pu platter special with the drinks specials. I always came home missing a sock, or an earring."

Owned by Miss Kiki, with help from her sister Gigi, Kiki's Tiki was known for not always doing what was expected and for having drinks that could not be found in nature. It did a few things very, very well. The menu wasn't carved in stone, except for the Hawaiian plate lunch brunch on Saturdays and Tori Katsu on Tuesdays. You could spear your own fish straight out of the tank. Pictures were extra. While generous, Miss Kiki knew there was money to be made and health inspectors to be bribed. She would find ways to ease a few more dollars out of customers. After a couple of drinks it was very easy. In an early promotion she advertised: *Last Friday of every month, fire breathing and juggling!!!* Six months later: *"This will be the last Friday, because of fire codes."*

In a rare interview (one of only two ever done), the legendary Miss Kiki said of the promotion, "It was a miracle we lasted that long, but it helped that the fire marshal was dating my sister. It came to an end when he found out that she was also seeing a local judge who happened to be his ex-brother-in-law."

Miss Gigi was quick to add, "I never said a word to him about work or what I did in my spare time. I have always been supportive of those who serve the public. He was just mad that I wouldn't go to the firemen's picnic with him. I had a show to do."

Miss Kiki: "The place was always one step away from being shut down for pushing the limit."

Miss Gigi: "Which is why everyone would want to see us."

Miss Kiki: "One time we let a spider crab walk around on a leash. Then there was the time we thought everyone would want a flaming drink, and it set off the sprinklers."

Miss Gigi: "So we declared an impromptu wet t-shirt contest for all men. Women judging."

Miss Kiki: "The winner got a puffer fish in the tank named after him, and limitless drinks for a month."

They wanted the place to be social, and not just with drinks and spring rolls. They held a science fair to see who could build the best volcano. It took three days to clean up and after that they decided to just build a volcano near the bar that would erupt every hour. There was also a ceremony involving Miss Kiki's neighbour Barb, who was kind of into mystical stuff and came to bless the place—but then she saw their mechanic who had not fixed the strange sound that their Buick Lesabre kept making while charging over 2,000 dollars in repairs. The mechanic developed a mysterious rash.

Miss Kiki said of the experience, "Normally I would have offered discounted drinks to any customer who ends up with a strange rash on our premises, but I heard the strange noise the car made and he was banned for life. He deserved that rash." Another well-known figure banned for life was Chevy Chase, who owed a bouncer about $1,500 from a poker game. No one liked him anyways, as he tipped the servers poorly.

The favourite regular was an older guy named Paul. Known to the bartenders as Mr Bliss Street, he liked scotch, coffee, quiet and his usual stool. He was one of three people who was allowed an open tab for the entire month. If you mentioned certain poets in his presence he might buy you a drink.

One of the most famous drinks there was the cocktail offered if it was someone's birthday. The Vicki-Kiki (named after the owner) had pineapple juice, passion fruit nectar, vodka with gold flecks, Ceylon Arrack, and white rum. As you drank it, the bartender would announce, "You will be a gold god." Usually what would happen is that the birthday boy/girl would end up passed out in a booth with a couple of palm fronds covering them like a blanket. (And a free cab ride home.)

One of the strangest nights that no one can entirely confirm is the evening that Sammy Davis Jr appeared. He was known for being quite talented at the hula (and incredibly respectful of the trained dancers who would appear on stage twice a week. According to one dancer, the famous tap dancer/actor/singer/activist spent a few years off and on studying the dance form with a *kuma hula*). Afterwards he went into the kitchen and cooked for a whole shift and then disappeared into the night. No one was sure what he was cooking. He didn't cook a single thing from the menu. He just cooked and people ate whatever he created. Everyone asked for more, but no other chef could recreate what he made.

Because he told Lena Horne that "they were good people", every once in a great while she would sit in with the band and sing. Everyone would end up a near sobbing mess when she would sing "What Is This Thing Called Love?". Even the busboys would come out to listen.

The true Queen of the Tiki was Miss Kiki and Gigi's mother. When she would show up, the cooks would come out, hug her, and complain about her daughters, then promptly make her a prime rib sandwich. It was never on the menu, but the chef would always make it because he liked her so much. Then, if she was up to it, she would play a little Gershwin on the piano. For laughs she would play a reverent version of "Jingle Bells", just to get a few laughs out of the customers, before telling stories about her misspent youth. Eventually, as it happens in all chaotic fun places, money, time and changing tastes made Kiki's Tiki disappear into the ether like Brigadoon. But if you have a rum punch and some bacon-wrapped scallops on a stick, you might suddenly hear "Midnight at the Oasis" being sung by two sisters as the volcano goes off announcing the start of Happy Hour.

ℰ

LOW-PRESSURE SOUP FOR A HIGH-PRESSURE SITUATION

You get ideas sometimes. (At two in the morning I begin to seriously think about how I ought to take up tap-dancing.) You take up an exercise routine, or learn to paint with oils. You are an adult and you want to expand your world and tend to your soul—and then it goes awry. Let's assume you are like me and decided to get a veg box. It is organic! You will be supporting the local farmers! You will stop letting that sad salad mix become soupy! We're eating vegetables now! They begin to send you some. Look, there is a biodegradable box on your doorstep, and there are unwashed wholesome vegetables that have had Plutarch and 19th century romantic poetry read to them as they grew in those beautiful fields. Green things. Vain things. Kale, butternut squash, carrots that are covered in dirt in a way to make them admirable like Gabriel Oak. Maybe some exotic purple sweet potatoes, and cauliflower. Always the cauliflower.

I must pause and ask what British people are doing with their cauliflower? They seem to buy a lot of it. I see them in grocery stores with their cauliflower. They don't seem like the sorts that prepare it in some continental Roman fashion with breadcrumbs. While England does love curry, I can't imagine all the pale Daves and Heathers are creating a bit of tandoori cauliflower. Maybe they are. Please write on a postcard what you are doing. I suspect a lot of cauliflower cheese—which is good, but I need to eat other things. I end up with a lot of cauliflower, and frankly the cauliflower seems to sit in the fridge judging me. "Yes, I know I am not glamorous like those Japanese greens over there. Why do you keep pushing me to the back?" It threatens to go off as a form of revenge. And you can't have that because, sweet Maude, you have this vegetable box. You have paid a sum for it, so things must be used. We are going to help you with this modern middle-class malaise.

What are we going to do? We are going to make soup. You have it for supper on a Sunday night, with some bread you have been ignoring as well. This will be inexact like everything else you are doing with your life. It is all good intentions and reckless improvisation, but for once it will work without someone having a shouting match. Maybe.

You poke about in the crisper and pantry. You have a butternut squash or a sweet potato or two. The regular kind. (Not the high-falutin' purple ones.) That head of cauliflower, an onion, a couple of carrots, and the last of the kale. (You thought you were going to juice or make smoothies. You didn't. You had another cup of coffee and a cold crumpet. It is okay.)

There is going to be some form of soup. Peel and dice your onion and sauté that in a bit of olive oil. Add a few cloves of smashed garlic. At least three. More like six. We aren't fragile people who feel uncomfortable in the presence of garlic. Let things soften. Now you will toss that into a pot with a peeled and chopped-up squash. (Or sweet potato. I know this is inexact but just accept this. Do I look like a wound-up television chef who wants to explain in numbing detail why you must have this many ounces? No. I am just a woman trying to make dinner and use up these damn vegetables.) Plus the carrot and torn apart kale. Toss it all in there. Chop up the cauliflower in a haphazard fashion. Just dismember that thing and put it in the large pot. (Side note, you can also do this in a crockpot.) Add some thyme, a bit of paprika, some salt, pepper, hey, even that tarragon looks fun. Oh look, you dig in the fridge and find a few green onions. Chop them up and add them in.

Then pour in four cups of vegetable stock. (You might need more. Things happen.) Bring it up to a simmer over medium heat and let it cook for a few hours. (If you are using the crockpot, let it cook on high for about four-ish hours.) Every so often as you walk by, give it a stir and see how things are cooking down. Maybe taste the stock. Go lie on the sofa and text a friend who might be entertaining and have good gossip. Or maybe it is your job to offer moral support. "Don't stab him. It will mean cleaning up a mess." "You need to fool around with them. For me. For the world. Also I want a full report. Wear your stockings. Trust me." Then after a few hours of not living up to your potential, go and check on that soup. Maybe it needs a bit of chervil because you have it in the cupboard and it is one of those things that tastes good when added at the end. If you have anyone coming over, you can make a point to mention that ingredient. Though they might find you annoying. So don't mention it, actually. Just feel pleased with yourself if they ask what spices you used.

Now come some serious decisions about this soup. Some people like smooth soup. Others like chunks and bits and pieces and want it to be a treasure hunt. It is vegan in this state. You can leave the soup as is, serve it up with some grilled bread, and a bit of cheese or whatever you find in the cupboards. If you have an immersion blender, or a regular blender or a food processor (we like options), you can take the soup and purée it. Maybe thin it with a bit more stock. (A mushroom stock would give it a slightly richer flavour and keep it vegan if that is a concern.) If you want a little dairy, you can purée it and then add a bit of cream or yogurt. Maybe serve it with a bit of chevre on top, where it can slowly melt into the soup and make it really pretty.

You may find yourself with a lot of soup. And you can only feed so many people. You can freeze it. You can ignore it with little worry. Then one January you will have another moment of organization and poke around the freezer and find that container of soup and think, "Yes, there is dinner sorted." Or maybe your SAD is out of hand and trying to make a whole complete dinner sounds like trying to cross the Siberian steppes. Thaw it out, warm it up, and maybe add something else to it. (Croutons, bits of bacon, some mushrooms.) You are fed and won't end up with SAD-related rickets. Sure, months later you find out you can substitute the cauliflower for something else and you have been stuck in this cauliflower purgatory for no good reason, but at least now you have soup.

C

CHOOSE YOUR OWN ADVENTURE

Pretty rose-coloured cuts of topside and flank steak were lording it over the modest shin and leg meant for stews. Brisket was nestled up against the short ribs with their mottled appearance reminiscent of archipelagos on antique maps. None of these crimson pieces of meat appealed to Cosima. She glanced at her ticket. Three numbers ahead of her before she had to choose something.

Cosima had promised to cook for him. She could cook easily for friends or family. But to cook for him would mean exposing herself when he took those first bites and tasted her feelings for him. She peered at the case containing the poultry. Quail, goose, squab, even a pheasant in a showy exhibition—making it clear that this place catered to aspirational sybaritic tastes that recalled an age of school ties and heavy claret drinking. This left the chicken and the duck. Cosima could make an ardent declaration of admiration with a roast chicken. She told herself, "Not the duck. All that fat requires a taste for fatalism." A duck called for a different sort of confidence, ease with one's kinks. She knew the chicken could make someone submit their love and appreciation to the chef. The duck was for when she wanted to make a man offer his soul, and in exchange she would hand over anything he desired. Her knickers, her heart, her tears. Anything.

The butcher called for number thirty-six. Two to go. Cosima knew she could roast the chicken in her sleep. A bit of butter and salt to make the skin crisp. (A tiny test to see if they appreciated good things.) A few herbs to add some depth of flavour and aroma, and garlic. Always garlic (ideally a whole head). Anything less than four or five cloves was an insult to the bird and everyone in the room. If he found the garlic overwhelming, she knew to not serve dessert, or to put on Marvin Gaye.

The duck did look pretty. But there was so much pain and risk in cooking the duck. It was messy and required more prep than an evening with the Marquis de Sade. You couldn't just pop it in the oven and not consider it for a while. There would be teasing the excess fat away from the body, pouring boiling water over the bird—the best way to get that beautiful crackly amber skin. Then she would have to be patient and wait for it to cool before piercing the skin all over and rubbing in salt, pepper, thyme, and cinnamon. It would be laid gently, breast side down, to cook. Later, the fat had to be drained (that beautiful gold, which could be used to roast the vegetables so that the entire meal was permeated with the scent and flavour of the duck, and Cosima's lust) before the duck was turned over on its back to continue roasting. As it cooked, they would hear the increasing volume of the sizzling fat, knowing the smoke was likely building in the oven. Everything on the verge of catching alight before being pulled out at the last possible moment. A pan full of excitement with fat erupting and splattering on any available surface, be it the duck or Cosima's bare skin. (A few light burns were good to show a dining companion as proof of devotion in wanting to feed someone well.)

"Thirty-seven!"

Cosima thought to herself, "Chicken. Definitely the chicken. I don't want to scare him off. For all I know he might only like white meat and the dark pink flush of duck meat might be too much." She knew that not everyone had the romantic sensibility to seek out the experience of being on the edge of tears or smiles tasting the steak-like texture of the breast, or the tender gamey leg with meat that slid off the bone like a silk stocking. It would be like listening to Chopin or Liszt and feeling helpless to every sensation.

"Thirty-eight!"

It was her turn. She told the butcher, "I think I want the chicken, but the duck looks good too."

He said, "How many are you serving? The duck is ideal if you are only serving two people; otherwise you might need a couple of them. The chicken is on special."

The chicken did look good. The chicken was easy to appreciate, like pretty ballet steps, or the unchallenging music of Telemann.

Cosima said, "Give me one duck, please."

Nothing but fearlessness and decadence tonight.

As Cosima walked out the door and heard the bell ring she thought, "I hope he isn't a vegetarian."

℮

IN TOO DEEP:
A RECIPE FOR BROWNIES

Brownies do not have to be a complicated affair. Let's imagine that you want to graduate from the box version, but you aren't quite ready to engage in the scavenger hunt for artisanal ingredients. (Most people do not want to spend their time looking for teff.) Maybe ten minutes of effort and a little time in the oven, and you will have bar cookies to bring elation to a wide cross-section of people. But before one can experience or provide pleasure, one must submit to a bit of labour.

Preheat the oven to 360°F/180°C and grease and flour an 8"x8" pan. Pyrex is good, because, as you know, Teflon leads to a lot of questionable decisions. I am sure that Jonathan Franzen was under the influence of Teflon when he wrote that awful article in the *New Yorker* about Edith Wharton. Trust me.

Do you have a saucepan? Why not? They are useful. You don't need a lot of pots and pans, but a saucepan will take care of most things in life. Get your saucepan and pop that onto the stove. Over low-medium heat you will melt four ounces of butter and four ounces of chopped-up bittersweet chocolate. There are people who prefer unsweetened chocolate, and some who like milk chocolate. These are your brownies. I go with bittersweet because it is a good middle ground—useful for uniting people with varying opinions on Genesis (the band, not the book). I know it is tempting to turn up the heat a bit, but you don't want to accidentally burn the chocolate. The acrid flavour and scent will hang about with you for a while, and no one wants that. Stir the chocolate and butter a bit to keep things moving and even.

Just as the last bit of chocolate is on the verge of melting you need to remove the saucepan from the heat. (Don't forget to turn off the burner. Not that I know anything about that.) Yes, you can melt the butter/chocolate down in the microwave, but again you run the risk of burning the chocolate, and it is actually a little fiddlier, what with the starting/stopping of the microwave to check things/give it a stir. You might end up using more bowls and utensils, and one wants to make things simple and get to the brownies as soon as possible. You may have to work quick, as there might be physical threats being made in the next room regarding some people's opinions about post-Peter Gabriel Genesis. You can only distract people for so long by bringing up the fact that "Abacab" had some cool ideas on it. Not that every single one worked, but they were trying a lot of different things. If you want to keep the peace just remind everyone that "Invisible Touch" wasn't Genesis at their best. That will get you a lot of nods and someone will put down the vase they were about to throw.

Your butter and chocolate have melted. Add one cup of sugar and stir it in. (You can drop it to three-quarters of a cup of sugar if you are using milk chocolate.) Then beat in two eggs and one tablespoon of vanilla. We are nearly at the finish line.

Stir in three-quarters of a cup of flour and half a teaspoon of salt. Just mix it enough so that the white streaks disappear. If nuts are your thing, mix in one cup of chopped nuts. Your choice. You know what you like. Pour the batter into the Pyrex pan and put that into the oven and bake for about 25 minutes. They should be set, with maybe a hint of a crack around the edges.

These are pretty fudgy brownies and quite dense. I would suggest letting them cool at least ten minutes so that it is easier to cut them out of the pan. Usually it is enough to make 16 brownies. Everyone will enjoy the brownies and agree that they are fantastic, and that one can always find new and exquisite treasures when listening to "Selling England by the Pound" for the millionth time.

THE BORSCHT OF MIRRA,
MAGDA, AND MIMI

I only went to Poland because I followed the advice of an aunt. Upon my marriage to the count, my aunt Leonilla had me to tea to see how I was taking to wedded life. She liked to say that she had been fortunate enough to be widowed before the age of thirty. She had done her duty very well in providing two male heirs and could enjoy her grand apartments in peace, without the pressure to remarry.

She said, "You are like your mother. You married a weak man. You may be offended by my words, but I am not concerned about that. He will be as faithful as a cat that scrounges three meals from three different cooks and still comes home claiming hunger. You are expected to thrive on the few crumbs that he might offer you out of duty. You aren't allowed to be hungry for anything else except those crumbs. Seek out your own satisfying meal. Your Aunt Zinaida finds nourishment in her faith, but you don't seem like the sort to collect icons, or holy men. Give Fyodor the heir, and then have others to please you. Don't just choose counts and princes. They are only available when it suits them. Be shrewd. A man at different stations can be useful. Make sure they share a feature with your husband." Aunt Leonilla offered cake and added, "No one asks about Felix's strange eyes—his jaw is just enough, like his dear departed papa."

Aunt Leonilla was correct about the man I married. Fyodor was dashing, and charming. He was dashing and charming with every woman. (And some men.) I was chosen because I came with property and the right family name. I never had the chance to provide an heir that had the right ears, but Mirosław saved my life. It was his sisters who gave me the means to keep living for the rest of my life. Within a few days of arriving in their home, I was shown into the kitchen and Mirosław's eldest sister Sora said, "Mirek isn't here to spoil you, your highness. Time to help with the soup." She handed me an apron and told me to cut beets. I mimicked her actions as she cut other things for the day's cooking. My hands were soon stained in the bright pink juice of the beets. Halina, the younger sister, teased when I complained: "See, we will turn this White Russian red yet."

Sora directed me to put the beets and garlic into a large bowl with salt and water. She added a small piece of stale rye bread and covered it with a muslin cloth. "Now we wait for the sour to wake up." It was our weekly ritual. Monday the sour was made, for the Friday soup.

❧

I learned to cook in Poland. I learned to season in Paris. Before Poland I never went into the kitchen. I never had to. Then I had to. That isn't true. I had as a child. For a time I was allowed to be with the other children on the estate. I would help them with their chores, or we would go foraging in the forest. It was work for them but a kind of play for me. The children didn't object to my presence. They thought I was simple, as I spoke Russian like a baby. Like when encountering any other baby, the children loved that they could teach me words and things about my environment. I would repay those hearty Russian words and eventual sentences they gave me, by offering them *amuse-gueules* of the French I spoke with my father and tutor, or the clipped bites of English I had learned from my nanny.

After being "at work", I would follow them to someone's *izba*. We would be fed bread or soup while someone's mother or babushka would continue to poke the fire in the stove, while tending to a baby, or returning to spinning. It wasn't until I was older that I understood that the women knew who I was and didn't say a word about me taking their family's bread or soup. Maybe they couldn't object to my presence. Or they pitied the girl—though there was nothing to pity. Yes, I had lost my mother (she was a delicate woman who lived on a chaise, gossiping with family about court life, when she wasn't preparing to attend a social occasion), but I had everything compared to these people. The only comment ever made was by the father of Galinka (one of the older girls), who came home to find me eating the last of the cheese. He asked if he was going to receive payment for the loss of his supper. Galinka defended me by saying I had brought home mushrooms and had fed the ducks. He said, "Your mother cannot make cheese from that. Her highness should return to her dacha where they have her supper waiting."

It was my last visit to a kitchen for many years. My Aunt Zinaida arrived to see to my upbringing. She ended my games of being a peasant. My father was a man who had other places to be. He preferred the long weekends at other people's estates, and the ballet where his latest mistress was performing. Children were to be tended to by women, and servants. Even after he remarried that German countess, I rarely saw him. They were on an endless tour of spas, and visits to friends in warmer climates. His letters would make regular references to her "gentle constitution and digestion that are in need of more sun," and not to the fact that she had been twice divorced and wasn't welcome at court.

I did keep the Russian. There was formal literary language as taught to me by a governess. Galinka, who came to the house as a maid, kept me in the dialect. Galinka's dropped vowels were the same fun play I had found in picking mushrooms. Aunt Zinaida thought it was vulgar when she heard me speaking Galinka's words. My aunt had me recite poetry in French or English to try

45

and train my tongue away from common words. My tongue had discovered a comforting if unrefined flavour.

I treated Galinka like a doll and insisted she come with me as my maid when I married. I did not consider whether she wanted to come away from her family, or if she had a sweetheart. I wanted my friend who did as I wished. The one who laid out my clothes, made my hair pretty, and let me gossip about family and court life. Galinka had a gift I did not possess: ease with all men. I was aware of my position and could flirt in a capricious manner, but Galinka had the ability to manage them like they were greedy dogs who wanted everyone's supper, offering little titbits to satisfy them for a moment while removing what they might actually want— even if it wasn't theirs to take. I didn't recognize her cleverness to survive until I hurt her. Galinka had been the one who led me to Mirosław. No, that isn't true either. My own petty rage led me to him. She pointed him out to me as the new groundsman on the estate and told me how he read books, and that she thought that his moustache was very attractive. They would spend time together on her afternoon off. She said he had opinions about politics and told her about his family. Sometimes he would kiss her. In the evening we were like two girls as she did up my hair, or helped me in the bath, me offering chocolates in exchange for details. I wasn't going to allow her to marry, as I didn't want to lose her, but I was pleased that she had a sweetheart—even if he was just a bookish Pole.

Then the outside world brought muddy chaos into the home. The war happened and Fyodor went off to fight and was rudely injured and came home to recuperate. All that worthless charm. I never said anything about Fyodor's taste for every woman in his midst until I saw him touch Galinka. I sent her to bring him coffee as he did nothing but complain in my presence. (Always the same things: the estate, the war, money, why he didn't have an heir yet.) It wasn't just that he grabbed her by the waist and was familiar with her. It was noticing how she smiled and seemed to be amused by his presence. I was disgusted by him for meddling with a servant. I knew it was one thing to bother one of the other maids, but not my maid. (Especially after the criticisms about a lack of a baby. Fyodor didn't seem to understand that he needed to visit my bed more than once in a while. Stumbling into my bedroom drunk and passing out wasn't going to produce a thing.)

I hated her for not staying in her place, and for being accommodating. Some take their marbles home. I chose to kick everything into the gutter and let no one play. I knew I would not give him a baby, and I would take away her happiness. When Fyodor returned to lead his soldiers to their doom, I began my own campaign. Taking advantage of Galinka being shut away in a room sewing things for me, I sought out her Mirosław. I offered him books from the library, and myself. He took both. Gladly. I was giving away things that didn't really matter much to me. He gave me easy attention. He now told me of his family, his opinions, and his view of the world.

Then came the letters from Fyodor telling me that things were not going very well. By then I ignored most of his letters. Then came the letter informing me that he was being held somewhere in the East. Everyone was going somewhere or disappearing. Both of my aunts decided to accept my father's invitation to stay in Denmark at his wife's family home. Fyodor's parents chose to go to Sweden. His mother's last words before leaving on the train were that I ought to wait for her son's instructions. Then the imperial family was gone. While Galinka began to sew gems into my petticoats, Mirosław told me he could find a way to take me across the border to his family.

I asked, "What of Galinka?"

"She should stay. This is her land. Come with me. Your husband is gone. You can finally be useful."

He spoke of a new life where I could support his cause and be free. He liked to tease me and tell me that I was a simple ornamental bird in a cage. He wanted to open the door and let me find my own branch to land upon, preferably one that was connected to his. My Galinka who packed for me was to stay. I told her that Mirosław was taking me to my family and that I would send for her when I could. I told her to take anything in the house that might be useful and we would settle up later.

She smiled and said, "Mirra, you already took the man, so I might as well take the silver or that pretty talisman, and we will be even, yes?" We were children once again. No more honorifics. She was the older girl explaining what everything around me was. I had taken enough from her and she didn't think the man was a good steal on my part. She sat me down while pinning up my hair and didn't let me speak.

"He will find another who is more valuable. His charm and charisma are about as useful as *zefir* in the middle of a heatwave. Don't be a fool and tell him all of your secrets." She pushed that last pin into my hair without any sweetness, for her role was over. It was agreed that I would give her a letter of reference, a month's wages, a bracelet she had always favoured, and my other sable coat. I took the man and left Mirra behind. Crossing the border with my new papers I was now Magda, playing the part of his wife. A wife who was to be left with his mother and two sisters, Sora and Halina, because Mirosław was to take up the cause in Eastern Galicia.

I was his prize after his time among the Bolsheviks. Now his fellow Poles called. But what did it matter; there was stock to make. Always stock on Thursday.

❧

The first time we made stock I was surprised that Sora put pork ribs into the pot. I handed her my badly chopped onions and carrots and said, "Your people don't eat that."

"My people? Magda, not everyone is frum. It is what the butcher had. I take what I can get when it is cheap. I am surprised you know what we eat, since your people don't want us about."

Sora took me in because her brother asked her to, but I was not a guest. I could have gone on to my father in Denmark, but I found myself at play once again. Their mother wasn't well, so I was to help care for her. It was almost like my daily visits to my mother as a child. I would listen to her gossip about family, admire her pretty shawl, and make sure she had her tea or necessary dear objects. In between I learned how to make beds, use an amusing sweeper for the carpets (I loved that because I would dance about the sitting room with it) and help as best I could in the kitchen. There weren't fun chores like eggs to collect or mushrooms to forage, but helping Halina or Sora with the marketing was close to it. To keep me safe and to make sure their mother asked fewer questions, I was Magda. Sometimes in public I was Magda the cousin, occasionally Magda the fiancée, and when Mirosław would return from Galicia on whatever form of leave he had, I got to play Magda the wife. That part was the most fun, if the most rare. Sometimes in bed we would talk about being those characters, "husband and wife", but it was a game. He was around as often as any other man I had ever known, immediately expecting adoration while demanding freedom. (They never asked if a woman might want those things too.) I wasn't too sure if I still had my proper husband. I wasn't entirely sure who one wrote to, as there was this new government that didn't share much, and there was my mother-in-law, who was about as friendly as the Bolsheviks when it came to answers. (I hadn't bothered to write to her, as she would ask what I had done with the family silver. I didn't want to tell her it was somewhere across the countryside in possession of the kitchen servants, as it had seemed like the quickest way to pay them.) I could do little, so I simmered like the stock and let things be.

I wasn't forthcoming about the value of my underthings. (They stayed in my suitcase in the linen cupboard.) I had sold one small gem and would hand over money in dribs and drabs when I saw Sora making a stock with mushrooms instead of meat, and I knew that the accounts were squeezing everyone at the end of the month. The family did not have much money. Halina was a teacher, and Sora worked in a shop part of the time. The sisters didn't ask about the money but would nod when I handed it over to one of them as we went to the market. That was where my language lessons in Polish would take place. *Marchewka i cebula* for carrot and onion. *Czosnek*—garlic, which we used to flavour, and to keep us well. And the ever-present *ziemniak* (potato), which went into so much of what we ate. Soup, dumplings, and salads. Over and over. So simple and steady. Sometimes I imagined I was a character in a folktale, living in a simple cottage with a grandmother and two witch sisters. I liked to do this when I was helping Halina skim off the scum of the stock that had been cooking for hours and would tell her, "Now our special potion is ready." She would laugh at my game and say, "Who should we put a spell on? Maybe Pawel the baker so that he will take me out? Or that the head of the school sees reason to give me more money."

Skimming the stock was where we began to lay our wishes and speak of any anxieties. Their mother would leave her chair in the sitting room and come into the kitchen when it was time to strain the stock. She would be the one to remove the meat from the bones and put the bones to one side to be sold off. Ciocia (as I was told to call her) couldn't lift the full pot off the range anymore, but she would lay out the cheesecloth like she was preparing a baby's bed, then with a bit of help would ladle the stock bit by bit and strain it. She would make comments if it wasn't beautifully clear. Asking what we had put in it: had we forgotten the pepper or the bay leaves, or gotten notions about putting in things that didn't need to be in there? When it was warm outside, we would use some of the stock to make a sorrel soup. It was tart like borscht, but it tasted more like spring and of the longer light in the evenings.

Ciocia would ask after her Mirek (I was the only one who would call Mirosław by his given name). He was everyone's pet. Even Sora, who had opinions about her brother leaving them to chase ideas and play soldier in a war while leaving random women in their home, would speak of him like he was still a boy at school. Now and then he would send letters to us. Tender, boyish words for his mother; teasing comments to his sisters; rambling words about the war mixed with bits of passion about what we might do when it was all over. I was forgetting more and more about going to Denmark. There were things to do here. I began to know this little world of people in the town. Halina would tell me about her students, who I would see on the street (the ones who couldn't really afford good shoes, or books). Sora or Ciocia would mention in passing while making tea that some neighbour wasn't well or someone was struggling, like so many.

"She takes in laundry—has since her husband died—and her hands are bad with arthritis. I don't know how she keeps going."

"He can't seem to work. Some think he is lazy, but his wife says he isn't quite right in the head, ever since the war."

I looked at my bit of money when Sora was making the poorer stock that wasn't so clear and knew it was time to sell another gem. I took the train into Warsaw and sold a necklace. (I didn't mind so much about the necklace, as it had been a gift from Fyodor on the last birthday I saw him.) It wasn't enough to save the world, but I thought I could do something nice. I also came home with a new hat for myself, and trinkets for everyone. I gave my old hat to Sora because hers was so old-fashioned and frumpy. She may have been a spinster, but I told her, "You should still look like a stylish woman who may not want a man but could have one." She smirked and enjoyed trying on my hat at various angles while telling me I had a lot of opinions for a woman who couldn't be bothered to locate her husband. Ciocia loved her slippers and said she would last at least ten more winters to get full use out of them. Halina wasn't sure if she could wear her gloves to school without people whispering that she must have gotten that raise, but she did wear them out to the concert that weekend with Pawel the baker. I gave Sora plenty of money for the shopping, made sure that Halina could buy books for the children, and hired the lady to wash simple things that didn't require much scrubbing. I wrote to Mirosław, telling him of my good deeds. I wanted him to be proud of his ornamental bird. He wrote back asking for socks and questioning if the books would teach the children to be critical of the bourgeoisie, or if it was the same nonsense to keep them prisoners.

I wrote to my father to tell him I was in Poland. I received a short missive saying that there was little room, what with everyone else staying with them, and that he could only go to Biarritz this year as money was so tight. He said I should find my husband.

Letter writing didn't return much pleasure. I devoted myself to learning how to slice beets thin enough for Sora's approval. "Like matchsticks, Magda. Stop being afraid of having stained hands. It isn't as if the Tsarina is coming to tea anytime soon." Nothing was neat or tidy anymore. We would chop up vegetables and add them to the stock along with the meat, *zazharka*, and towards the end there was the beet sour that began it all, and the very last thing was a bit of cabbage. Ciocia would say, "You don't want the cabbage limp and sad. This soup is alive!"

I liked our foursome on Friday evenings. There were stories from the week, plans to make, and gentle teasing as we shared out the bread and sprinklings of dill. Sometimes others would come and eat with us. It would turn into funereal merriness over little glasses of wine, everyone remembering lost moments in time whilst trying to cobble together something good for the future out of these frayed memories. I would recall playing in the woods as a child, or the fun with Galinka as she taught me to curse. The countess was almost an imaginary figure. Mirra who had gowns by Worth, and her Galinka, and who had been everyone's pet. One night after much wine I brought out a ring that had belonged to my mother because the stone was the exact shade of the borscht after the sour cream had been stirred in. Everyone took turns wearing it and swanning about the kitchen. We laughed about losing it in the soup and how it would be a much better find than any coin in a cake.

Then Mirosław came home; his cause was won. Then I received word from my mother-in-law that Fyodor was gone. A martyr in her eyes. She asked after a piece of jewellery that belonged to the family, but nothing about my well-being. As there had been no heir, I was free, and almost respectable as a widow. I couldn't return home, but I could go anywhere. I liked playing house with my "cousins", but it wasn't my home. Mirosław made the next decision. Or his opinions made the next decision, as they were causing him trouble. Another gem had to be sold to release him. His opinions were becoming a little expensive.

While lying in bed and playing husband and wife, he said, "Little bird, we could go to Berlin!" I told him I didn't know much German, and why should we stay with our old enemies? He suggested London. I didn't like islands. They made me claustrophobic. He offered Italy, and I reminded him that is where writers go to die, and that he should live a little longer. I was Persephone, ready to return with spring.

§

Thus I came to Paris and added tarragon to the soup. Mirosław brought me along because I could speak French. I still had that youthful addiction to the charm of a man. Now I was to be a useful little bird who would darn his socks and allow him to write. I gave the borscht ring (as we took to calling it) to Halina as a gift as she was to marry Paweł the baker, and every married woman needs something that is hers alone. I left Sora a talisman. She didn't need protection, but like every other spinster she needed one thing that gave her the freedom to say yes or no. Ciocia gifted me with the secret of her *zazharka*. She told me that I could keep anyone alive with stock, and *zazharka*.

Mirosław had wanted a garret. "We need little. Just a bed. Maybe a table for my writing and for meals." A little pokey room where I would have spent my days cooking on a single burner, carrying water from a distance. I didn't need my dacha or the grand apartments anymore, but I demanded a kitchen with a sink. And more than one room. If he wanted to be fed, I needed a room away from him. We ended up with three rooms, a bed, a sofa, and a table and chairs. He had objected until he sat on the sofa and put up his feet and fell asleep. Another piece of jewellery had provided me with these comforts. I liked to play wife to Mirosław, but the secret wealth of my underthings remained with me. I only told him that my father made it possible for us to settle. Not a complete lie, as many of those pieces had once come from the family. Galinka did tell me that no man needs to know the absolute truth. The day she helped me pack she said, "Many of them think we are lying; the others use the truth against you. Keep the important things to yourself." I kept thinking of her as I wandered the noisy streets of the city. I wasn't a baby with language here. It was a familiar tongue, and still I borrowed her voice when I needed to be brave or manage the men in the markets.

Soup in Paris is different. Everyone wants a hand in its creation. From the man carefully picking out your carrots and onions, to the butcher selling you the cheap cut of meat. If you seem unsure, they will ask what it is for. They might offer that bored scoff of disapproval if it isn't their favoured cuisine. (One must expect and appreciate the fervour of their regional chauvinism.) If they come to respect you (because you don't complain too much about their prices, or you smile at their coarse flirting) they will find you just the thing. The dark-eyed man who often sold me onions and beets told me that soup was nothing without tarragon and gave me a bunch one day. He said it wasn't afraid to have flavour, unlike its Russian cousins. I offered him mock offence and said my soup was plenty strong and had flavour. He smiled and said, "This will give it tenderness. There isn't enough of that." His flirting was never crass.

On the floor above us lived an Italian woman, wife of a French doctor who worked all hours. She would stand at her balcony, often with a small child pulling at her skirts, watching the world and commenting to people as they passed by. She appeared to know everyone. One day she saw me coming along with my basket from marketing and called out that I seemed to be cooking for the world, as it always looked so heavy. She invited me up for coffee and to show her my basket. Letizia introduced herself and her young son Enzo as she prepared coffee. She offered pieces of her life story while yelling out to her son to stop climbing about on the furniture, but she was keener to share morsels of gossip about people in our building.

"Ignore their shouting. They always seem near divorce until they go to Normandy each August and are lovers once again."

"He claims to be a writer, but I think he does something as a spy. He keeps strange hours and never removes his hat—even when indoors."

Once we had our little cups and enough sugar, she asked what I was cooking, as she could often smell something and it made her curious because it wasn't familiar. I invited her to dinner on Friday and told her to come early so that I could show her what I was making. When Friday came, she arrived with wine, a well-scrubbed and tidy Enzo, and a lot of chatter. When it came to the *zazharka* she was amused by the parsnip and the beets.

"You are not from the south."

After dinner, she said, "The borscht tastes of you. It is from far away and has a few secrets. A soup that has lived." She offered to show me how to make her family's *soffritto*. "It has its own warmth."

We took to going back and forth to each other's apartments to cook for each other as our men were often away. Hers to heal maladies and mend broken bones; mine to build a new world free of tsars and make it pregnant with unions. (He seemed to spend much of his time in bars with his fellow agitators.) Often we had Enzo running around us with a tin toy train I bought him as his reward for finishing his meals at my home. We became Letu and Mimi to each other. And every Friday there was borscht, and Letu's biscotti with coffee.

❧

It was while walking with Letu through the Jardin du Luxembourg one Wednesday before going to the market that my old world popped up like an impromptu sideshow. For there was my cousin Felix of the strange eyes, along with another couple I remembered from social occasions. My aunt had told me that they had married because he needed money and she wanted a bigger title, but both had overestimated what the other had coming to them, and now they were stuck with one another.

"Cousin Mirra. How long have you been in Paris? This isn't your Galinka. Did she run off with the Reds? She was always uppity."

There were so many questions to answer. I tried to introduce Letu. Felix teased me saying he wasn't surprised that I still had a maid. There was an invitation to tea, cards given out, and promises of more talk soon, but they were off to an opening, and did I know the Grand Duke had returned to Paris? After kisses, the circus was gone as quickly as it had appeared. Letu looked at me and said, "Mimi, who are you?"

Everyone was loosely communist then, including Letu and her husband Yves. Everyone would be generous with the cheap wine and talk of throwing off the masters. To many, Russia was the future. When everyone would become excited, I would return to the kitchen. I couldn't add anything to the conversation, but I could to the soup. I added my own private thoughts along with my modified *zazharka* that Letu had influenced. When Mirosław would make comments to others about me being his little white *oiseau* that he snatched away from the aristocracy as a prize, I would add a little more sour to the soup at the end. Politics made everything bitter to me. I had to have something that tasted kind. I wasn't that useless little bird anymore. I made sure we ate while he wrote his articles for all those journals that didn't pay very much (and that I edited because his French was very uneven).

In the park, I smiled at Letu and said, "In Russia, a countess. In Paris, a widow. Let's go home and have coffee."

Letu pointed to herself and said, "In Italy, a nurse. In Paris, a housewife. Let us have cake at mine. But first the shopping. I promised Enzo I would try and find him apricots."

Her only question over coffee was whether I had had my own maid. I told her, "Yes, and I never paid her what she was truly worth."

Curiosity made me seek out my people. I wanted to see what I had missed. I braved tea with Cousin Felix and the other exiles one Tuesday at someone's apartments. Everyone who still had furs were wrapped in them. Some were like mannequins in the latest fashions; others were trying to make do with tea dresses from before the war. It was more like a reception after a funeral. People were in mourning—somewhat for loved ones, but mostly for the old life. They had the worst case of nostalgia. They should have been quarantined. You would have thought they would have been in a better state, being in Paris. They spoke the language, they liked the culture, and the French liked theirs. I teased a count who was moaning and said it wasn't that bad, as the French did adopt *service à la russe*. He merely turned away and asked for more tea. Then there were those who were trying to figure out who might be good for a loan or would be generous with a house in the south of France.

"Did you escape with anything?"

"Of course, you still have a maid. It must be pleasant to have the means and the comforts."

"I keep trying to get my property. The lawyers say it may take some time."

Even Felix seemed caught up in this belief that all of this was temporary. I made a few attempts at being welcoming by inviting people to tea or luncheon at my apartment (when I knew Mirosław would be out). Comments would be made about how adorable it was that I lived so simply, and they knew someone's English or Danish cousin who had a house for sale that would be perfect for me. Her Serene Highness Princess Irina thought Letu was my housekeeper and kept asking her for things even after I corrected her. Another eyed a vase and asked about its value. They looked so disappointed when I said I had found it for a few francs in a flea market. Once Felix realised that lunch or dinner wasn't going to involve an invitation to Maxim's, he began to tell me he must consult his diary before making plans. What was left of home? Had I been scraping at empty plates hoping for another meal?

I missed the trees, the light, the fierceness of winter, and always Galinka. Everything else the Bolsheviks could keep and distribute as they saw fit. It was enough to manage life in my few rooms and gather help in my narrow kitchen to keep everyone going. I had the letters to and from Sora. From a great distance she offered help with cooking, while giving me her wry opinions about her brother. "Mirek will bring you gifts, but never the milk or the bread you asked for." She made me miss playing house as she shared the gossip from home. Another baby for Halina, pains in the joints for Ciocia, and the laundry woman's luck in finding a widower to keep her company. I kept inviting Sora to Paris, but she needed to care for her mother and help in the bakery.

I had Letu who watched out for others and the world. Even as she would bathe Enzo, she would have me read the papers to her. Letu's urgency was very much at her pace. She always insisted on at least one more cup of coffee before going out. She would pour it and tell me, "The world, like a man, always wants something, so you might as well have a little coffee before answering the complaints."

I was Mimi from the east with her odd soup that was beginning to feed more and more, as Mirosław took to bringing people home. Just like he had with me. This was the best side of him. He saw my ability and someone's need. Sometimes it was just for a meal; other times people stayed for a few days. He was generous in giving our dinner to others. My few wishes regarding him had to with the desire to have more than five minutes' knowledge of impending guests. Always a call from the bar to Letu, who had a telephone, and her leaning over the balcony: "Mimi, is there is enough soup? Do you have enough bread? I can bring you cheese." Then she and her family would appear with wine or beer and there would be more company. The soup began to change shape with the seasons. In the deepest of winter it was completely my soup. In the summer it might be cold, or it had the tomatoes or peppers of Spain that were brought to us by our most regular visitor, Eztebe, who liked to come into the kitchen with me and chat to me in his strange French. He would always help with the dishes or entertain Enzo with string tricks. Others would take up space and ask me for more wine. When it was spring, the dark-eyed man from the market would sell me sorrel, when we were tired after a long winter of the deep red soup. He began to tell me that my stock needed a proper bouquet garni, and always insisted upon the tarragon. I would tease him and say he should come to dinner before making such pronouncements. He would always say, "Madame, be careful, I might say yes one day," before sneaking a few shallots, or fennel, into my basket.

Then Mirosław brought me the most permanent form of company: a baby. Maybe he thought it would occupy me while he went off to follow the next adventure. He enjoyed the brief pride of telling everyone he was to be a papa and how we would have a boy to become a great worker and he would be called Grigory or Lev. (Mirosław didn't trust Georgians.)

Aurélie Galinka arrived to tell her papa he wasn't correct. She was the first female not to placate his feelings or wishes. Her cries would interrupt his writing, or she would take away the attention he had enjoyed when company was about. He began to spend more time elsewhere. But he always came home for Friday dinner. I found that was about as much of him as I enjoyed. He would appear with some vodka or pastries, pat Aurélie on the head, ask if there were letters for him, and tell me about the state of things in the city. When he would complain that there wasn't any meat in the soup that week (sometimes, like Sora, I had to make do with mushrooms in the stock, especially as more came to dinner), I would say, "Contribute to the soup and the committee will consider your needs."

Then came the week the dark-eyed man in the market asked, "When do I get to try this soup you are famed for? Your friend the Italian lady keeps telling me of its virtues and flavour." I told him, "I will need extra tarragon, then. And your name." Amal arrived that Friday with his mother Fatima and sister Sofia. They brought dates, and flowers. The peonies were a rare and deeply appreciated sight. Mirosław had a low opinion of cut flowers and didn't like them in the apartment. He felt they didn't contribute much to society when fields could be better used to grow food. Even after Eztebe pointed out how worker bees needed flowers, Mirosław balked and said, "They should learn to make do with more useful flowers."

The less he was about, the more the apartment became filled with my vision of the world. I had given away the small table for a larger one that held more dishes and more people. We gathered around it as we listened to stories of Morocco, where Fatima had come from. She spoke of *dwaz atay* that her mother would make for visitors; elderly Berber aunties who had tattoos on their hands, feet and face; and of meeting a French soldier who married her and brought her to France. She came and sat with me in the kitchen, holding Aurélie and singing to her as I cooked. Letu occupied Amal with a million questions about his produce stall, and his interests. (She told me later that he painted.) Everyone was lost in conversation, dinner and the interruptions of children wanting attention. It was like the warmth in those *izbas* I visited as a girl. Everyone brought their past to the table, but they were equally interested in the present. Over dates we all made plans to picnic when the weather was hot, to have tea with Fatima and Sofia, and to take the children to the zoo. And there were further invitations to return the following Friday. Like the soup, everyone had their part to add to the week.

§

Ciocia's slippers lasted ten years but she didn't. Mirosław went home to bury his mother. When he returned he brought a gift: Sora! After so many years apart she still had the hat I gave her and, even more dear, her eyes still showed the spirit of all her forthright opinions. Upon being introduced to her niece Aurélie she said, "I was right, Magda. Never the milk or bread you need. I am glad she ended up with your chin, and his eyes." After looking around the apartment she went into the kitchen and said, "How is the sour? When will we make stock?"

Sora was here to stay. She criticized my stock but liked the additions to the *zazharka*. She loved the markets and had me translate her opinions to Amal so that she could argue with him. Sora came alive on Friday nights. Even with the lack of French she kept everyone amused with her expressions. She was everyone's auntie. Eztebe would take her out and teach her the names of everything within the market and in the gardens; she would knit him mitts to keep him warm in the winter as he trimmed trees and tidied paths.

The writer that Letu felt was a spy invited Sora to a concert of Chopin. We learned he knew enough Polish from a dictionary to offer her a seat on the bus, and milk in tea. That concert brought us Klara. This slight Franco-Polish woman came at Sora's invitation to dinner. Following brief introductions, she spent most of the evening following Sora about. Chattering away in Polish, switching to French to answer Letu's questions about her work as an art instructor in a girls' school, and her marital status. While helping me to ladle the soup and pass it around, Letu said, "I like that they enjoy each other's company." I thought it was wonderful that Sora had a friend. Weeks later Klara was still coming to dinner every Friday; she and Sora would occupy each other's attention in one corner of the crowded room and assist each other with washing the dishes. Often they would push everyone else out: "It's too small. Go enjoy the wine and coffee." Letu said to me, "It isn't often two people find such affection like that. They are a good match." It truly made sense to me when someone put a record on the gramophone and people were dancing. I saw them in the kitchen; they were a couple of loving little starlings prancing about with each other, giggling over their private jokes, and shy kisses.

A few months later Sora announced that my house was well-run enough and that she was to go and live with Klara and keep house for her. Letu nodded and said, "You are lucky to find someone who does dishes with you. Most women don't have that." Still, they arrived every Friday—often with their little dog, Berthe, who was chased about by Aurélie, or held like a baby by Sofia, who would say to me, "Some aunties know to avoid the work of men." We would laugh and Amal would ask why I had so many secrets with his sister before pouring drinks for everyone.

Each week had its ritual, and each week would bring something or someone new. I kept my table open and made it stretch over the years. I couldn't shut out the hardness of the world all the time. Letu made sure of that with her weekly commentary about the state of the world. But I could bring warmth with dinner, sometimes a bed or sofa to sleep on, and give attention to everyone's strengths. Yet everyone knew only a piece of me. Curious Mimi who once had a maid, and would nod at a man in the park who was supposedly a grand duke. The one that Sora called Magda. The mama that refused to marry or live with papa for her own reasons.

I was good at not telling the whole truth until Aurélie was old enough to ask questions. She was insistent and could see through my vague answers. I began to have her help me make the borscht each week and in exchange I began to tell her about the little girl who was a princess. And her time in the woods with old women who were like Baba Yaga. Letu would listen as I told of heavy dresses worn at court, of women who were covered in gems. Of a photo of her grandmother who went to a famous ball that lasted three days, and everyone dressed in old-fashioned clothes. At dinner there would be recollections of the land, the skies, and the sleighs going through the snow to attend the ballet and opera. Over coffee and cakes I would tell them of Galinka and then pass the story on to Sora, who would tell of my helplessness in the kitchen. We would share the stories of each other. We would go to bed so full. Even as things became darker we would laugh.

Mirosław decided to disappear into the storming clouds that were Spain. It was another cause, and exploit. He followed Eztebe, who had reasons to return. Mirosław sent back one last gift before disappearing for good. Pilar arrived with Eztebe, both in a terrible state. His gentle nature was never meant for that violence, and she was quite pregnant and had walked through the mountains with him. Letu's husband Yves tended to them and I fed them. They didn't know where Mirosław was, but he had told them to come to me.

I knew that Pilar wasn't just a random woman my Mirosław had offered help to. It became certain when she gave birth to a boy with his chin and brows. I had Eztebe tell her, "Pick a name you like, don't let his wishes for Joseph come true."

Luis and Pilar stayed with us. Another sweet baby to pass about (Aurélie would take her brother out and show him off to everyone) and another friend at the table to gossip with over coffee and sweets. Eztebe adored Pilar. He took her and Luis on walks through "his" parks. He soon decided that my apartment was too crowded and asked Pilar to marry him. I didn't want to lose the company of her and Luis, but I could see how Eztebe's gentle love had wooed her. Mirosław had saved her and given her one delightful gift, like he had with me, but beyond that he could never be counted upon for much. I gave her a bracelet as her own. She always wore it on Fridays. She never mastered French, and I never spoke much Spanish, but we knew each other as odd sisters. She was the one who would come into the kitchen, taste my soup and know when it needed a little more seasoning, and exactly how much dill would make it perfect.

We had all this wealth. This family where children grew and adults complained of back pain, or of bosses that got in the way of our fun. We wandered through each other's homes. We had our plans to visit the sea, to attend a festival, to watch races and feed each other dinner. Fatima and Sofia would steal away Luis for trips to puppet shows; Letu would go with Pilar to a flower show to see Eztebe's latest effort. Sora and Klara would meet up with the spy upstairs to attend art exhibitions and improve their French and Polish. (Sora said they mostly laughed a lot and never improved their vocabulary.) Aurélie would tag along with Enzo and his friends like a mascot to catch football matches, and Amal would take me out each Wednesday to the cinema and then walk with me and recite poetry. I appreciated his attention, but I wasn't quite ready to wash another man's socks just yet. He would kiss me three times on the cheeks before reaching my lips and say, "My precious Mimi, dinner is enough. For now."

I continued to sell off gems when I knew people around me were in need. Once upon a time they were to save me; now I knew they could do good for everyone. My ancient underthings were picked apart in funny spots. Then came the day when all those men marched into the city, and I knew I would need those gems to do more than ever.

But for now I was going to stick to my week. It was Friday. Aurélie wept and asked me what we were to do. I said, "Everyone is coming over in a bit. People need to be fed and then we will take care of each other like we always have done. Ask Letu if she can bring extra wine. Now let's see if we have enough dill."

C

CORDIALLY YOURS

Pound cake is sincere and loyal. Like Jimmy Stewart, or Dame Judi Dench. You mention pound cake and people will say, "Don't mind if I do." Or, "I have always liked that." It can be familiar but still surprising. Let's bake and eat a cardamom citrus pound cake. Let that sincerity melt into the cake as you try and create something to show your personality.

I should mention that this isn't a pedantic pound cake that requires a pound of every ingredient—though I suspect that would be amazing.

Cream together 225 grams of softened butter with 200 grams of sugar. Crack five eggs (room temperature so that they mix well) and mix them into the creamed mixture one at a time. So much mixing, you say. Sincerity and loyalty don't come just like that. They have to be *earned*. And stop complaining. There's going to be cake. Then stir in half a teaspoon of vanilla, the zest of one orange and the juice of one lemon. If you want to really go wild (and I know you do) you can use a Meyer lemon or a Seville orange. It will provide you with the opportunity to bore your family and friends repeatedly over the course of the evening by pointing out that there is fancy citrus fruit in the cake. As if you had searched foreign climes to find a rare and exquisite piece of citrus to make your cake a true thing of glory versus going to the grocery store and seeing them on offer. Take this time to taste the batter. Not for quality assurance but just to take in the simple pleasures of butter and sugar.

In a separate bowl whisk together 250 grams of flour, half a teaspoon of salt and two teaspoons of ground cardamom. You will add the dry ingredients into the wet mixture and do this in thirds, giving everything a good stir in between each addition. It will be a thick batter. Pour into a buttered and floured loaf pan—9"x5" will work for you. Maybe you are one of those people with novelty moulds and can give your cake a whole other impressive dimension. Not that you are trying to ask for love via the medium of baked goods. Okay, maybe you are. Just a little bit. Sometimes you can't just say things out loud; all you can do is make things look like other things and hope that it impresses someone.

Bake in an oven at 325°F /160°C for about an hour. It should be golden. Do a quick toothpick test to make sure it comes out clean. Let it cool for an hour. Spend that time trying to write a poem that shows how much someone means to you. You may come to hate yourself and decide the cake will be enough. If someone can't tell how much passion they inspire in you—well, then they just aren't worth it. (These are the insecure stories we tell ourselves in our attempt to loosen the cake from the tin.)

The cake will smell good and won't be too sweet. It will be something nice with a bit of ice cream or fruit. You will hold your breath as someone takes that first bite and declares that it is fantastic. But do they taste your feelings? Were you able to slip it past them because you chickened out at the last minute? Some do, some don't. Let's distract ourselves from the pain with different ways to turn this cake upside down. You could always toast two pieces of pound cake and then spread them with Nutella and marshmallow fluff and call it a sandwich. You could also take those toasted slices of cake and put a slab of ice cream between them (something like vanilla bean) and then pour butterscotch sauce on top and eat it with a fork and knife. Because sometimes you have to take a perfectly nice little cake and do wanton things with it, since that someone else in the corner won't.

LENTEN STEAK
AND OTHER SPIRITUAL CONUNDRUMS

If you don't have fun the approved way then you are diluting the brand and have no business even being here. Amusement is reserved for those of a certain income bracket because they are good and righteous and know best how to have fun. You aren't supposed to try and seek out gratification if you are poor. You start getting ideas about equality, or begin to examine a belief system that casts judgement on who is truly worthy to experience a bit of diversion. Until the supposed gatekeepers of mirth and joy read a few sermons by Saint Basil, it is best to ignore their nonsense, especially when you see a couple of steaks on sale. It is the end of another long week. You are feeling the hum of anticipation that comes with it being Friday in later winter and noticing the sun didn't set until after 5pm. Some may have to work on Saturday, but there won't be any kids to wake for school; there may be a bit more time with that cup of coffee before going in for that shift, or tending to those errands. It may be Lent, but this moment in time has its own fizz and headiness.

Culturally I come from a religious tradition where, historically, the spiritual loopholes granted to the laity on practical matters made one wonder if an entire team of Jesuit-educated lawyers with a passion for *dégustation* were put in charge of writing the dogma. One can't eat meat on Fridays during Lent, but one can eat beaver, iguana and capybara. (Colonizing the New World meant that Europeans had to become creative about what to eat for dinner when fish wasn't available.) Just find a creature that dips its toes in a pond, and it can provide the faithful with the opportunity to avoid another Friday supper of fish fingers flavoured with the growing tensions of someone who gave up coffee for forty days. (We still look upon the Lenten season my mother gave up chocolate as the one that felt a thousand days long.)

Let's take ourselves away from esoteric culinary questions regarding aquatic mammals and wander back to the real world of Friday night freedom. You are finally home. You pop the steaks into the fridge and have a drink. Unless of course you gave that up for Lent—then I suggest making a Socialist Mule (ginger beer, lime juice, simple syrup infused with mint, and crushed ice. Mix it all together and everyone can enjoy a bit of it). One too many nights of tuna casserole, or soup during grey often dreary weeks where it seems like spring will never appear, can lead someone to consider how a pile of scampi and chips with extra curry sauce might be in line with humility and spiritual discipline. In the Book of Matthew, the poor in spirit (from the Beatitudes) refers to those who are humble before God. I am guessing Matthew never faced the temptation of an all-you-can-eat seafood buffet. Blessed are the poor in spirit unless there are seafood chimichangas on the menu.

Philosophical gymnastics can lead a person down many roads. Be it muskrat stew or, in my family's case, perfecting the art of cooking a steak at ten to midnight so that it was technically ready on Saturday. It may not have been entirely in the spirit of a period devoted to self-denial. Sometimes, if you are fortunate, you can cheat the devil by blessing something (as Pope Clement VIII did when he tasted coffee and found it to be so delicious that he wasn't going to give it up). But we can't always rely on that method. So we wait. We take part in the rest of the evening. Have a penitent meal (something with aubergine, to make everyone sigh or feel disdainful), read a book, escape from the conventions of pinching, respectable clothing (put pyjamas on and forget leaving the house because it is now our time). When I was growing up, this was when my family would come alive. We are all chaotic night owls who decide that eleven at night is the hour to begin a new project or creation. There would be sudden denials of sober puritan words from earlier in the day about going to bed at a reasonable hour because a film we loved had come on. Children who had gone to bed would reappear. Sitting on the edge of a chair, saying they just had a question, or needed water, and then they would return to bed. Promise. The weakest promise in the world once someone brought out ice cream or popcorn. It was around this time the steaks were removed from the fridge and allowed to sit for a bit.

Some of the best games are obstacle courses. Cheap steaks on a Friday night is a game with multiple elements. We ignored the monitors of indulgence and respected the borders of our particular liturgical calendar (even if it was a bit like children chanting, "I'm not touching you," with pointed fingers less than an inch away from Lent), but there was one final hurdle: the orthodox guards of cooking steak. The ones who write bombastic sermons on how the great unwashed don't understand which cuts of meat should be used, and if one doesn't employ their particular method of cooking, the rapture will befall humanity. *Lo, it is written, if you dare to cook a ribeye in a pan that isn't of cast iron, and fail to rest the meat for ten minutes afterwards, the sun darkens, and the moon becomes as blood.* We permit them to stand at their pulpit in their holy whites and stained checked trousers as they are filled with the spirit. It gives them pleasure, but it doesn't mean we have to sit around and give an offering. We can sneak out and make our own steak.

My family—defiant of time, respectability and dictated culinary canon—cooked steak like rational human beings. Around 11:45, the stove would be turned on, and someone would season the steak. (Salt and pepper is the preferred choice, as we were simple people who liked peanut butter sandwiches with pickle or raw onion. Regarding the onion, my mother was an aficionado of Hemingway and trusted him regarding sandwich fillings.)

Butter would sizzle in the pan as it melted. (If you have a cast iron skillet that is wonderful. If you don't, use what is in your kitchen. Life is a constant struggle and we must make do at odd hours.) We believed in butter as much as we believed in the communion of the saints. It had not failed us yet. (Let's quickly recognize Saint Lawrence, the patron saint of cooks, who was treated like a sirloin in his martyrdom. He was alleged to have said, "Turn me over; I am done on this side." Is this what they mean by too many cooks in the kitchen?)

Around this point the dog would be racing around at the scent of things. (She was a queer creature who feared bananas, loved cooked broccoli, and was patient when it came to baby ducklings nibbling on her ears.) The steaks (usually two, for while they were on sale, we were many) were cooked for about four or five minutes on one side. Some of us preferred steak medium rare ("Ah, an aristocrat," we would mutter to each other). Then the steak was turned and cooked for a few more minutes. That is it. No chips, no creamed spinach. (Both beautiful things but not required as we weren't eating supper.) Then the steaks rested for a few minutes. No putting it under a grill. No letting it rest while it listened to Pink Floyd's *The Wall*. The resting time was mostly needed to find forks and knives. "WHO was playing with the good silver in the garden ... again??" (No guilty parties will be named here, as we are not one to snitch on siblings.) And we had to check the clock. Was it time yet? Had we met Saturday? It was finally here!

We would carve small bites for the smallest children while reminding them that they had ice cream. "Yes, but I want another bite." They would have another bite. We might torture each other in other ways, but we were always generous about late night feasts. While we watched a late-night chat show, making our own commentary to each other, we were happy together. It was the cosiest time with the funniest people. It was always the best tasting steak. A little wickedness and impudence add a kind of umami not found on most shelves. The smaller children were sent to bed once the ice cream was gone and someone pointed out what time people had to be up in the morning. The dog was often given the bone or a bit of fat after staring at someone and drooling on their feet. Half-hearted noises were made about sleep.

"It is late."

"I know, but let's just watch this scene."

Eventually sleep won.

We didn't want to give in completely to the fire of sin, but we sure appreciated the warmth of that perilous mephitic heat.

ℰ

THE SUPER-SECRET
PECAN BAR MEETING

You have the cranberry sauce ready, the gelatin salad is in the back of the fridge setting up nicely (sure, everyone makes fun of it, but you know everyone will have a serving on their plate), and you are more or less ready for tomorrow—but you have that itch to make one more thing. Not quite pie, a slightly more decadent tray-bake, and not for the people watching football in the other room, or those who are supposed to entertain the kids. This is something for everyone who is going to be in the kitchen tomorrow.

Got a bowl and a fork? (Sure, you can use a food processor, but let's make this accessible to everyone, not just YOU, Cheryl.) If you have a fork and a bowl, then you can make the crumb base. Take your bowl and dump in two cups of flour, half a cup of sugar, six ounces of butter, and a dash of salt. Use your fork (or pastry blender if you have a few more kitchen items, or you are your Grandma who may have arthritic hands but can still wield a pastry blender like some kind of kitchen warrior, all while telling you her opinions about "Grey's Anatomy", her friend Helen's new boyfriend, and why you should cut your hair short because you are too old to have long hair) and just mix and blend until everything reaches a fine crumb state. It should be kind of sandy. Take that mixture and press it into a greased 9"x13" pan. And then pop it in the oven at 350°F/180°C for 15–20 minutes until lightly browned.

While that is going on, you can quietly rehash with your cousins, your mom, and Aunt Sharon about the last year and how exhausting it has been, even though there is that "no politics" rule at dinner. But it isn't technically dinner. And your idiotic Uncle Gary totally tried to violate the rule by showing up wearing a MAGA hat until your Grandma reminded him that he was raised to take his hat off indoors, and while he is welcome to be a savage in his own home, it doesn't work that way at her house. She returns shaking her head. "I thought I hugged him enough as a child. Apparently not. Who wants some egg nog?"

Now you get out a saucepan and put in one cup of brown sugar, one cup of corn syrup, four ounces of butter, and you stir that over medium heat until the butter melts and everything comes to a boil, like the last 4th of July family barbecue where your idiotic Uncle Gary kept calling his wife "Butterfingers" all afternoon after she dropped the dish of devilled eggs, and your mom tore into her brother by reminding him that Aunt Sharon was an incredibly talented phlebotomist at the local hospital and how people came up to her all the time to tell her how quick and painless Sharon makes things, so maybe he should apologize to his wife. Aunt Sharon later whispered to my mom, *thanks*, and confessed that she didn't vote for Trump like her husband thought. She voted for Hillary and was in a secret Facebook group devoted to Hillary Clinton.

Now back to your pecan sugar topping. In a small bowl you crack the four eggs and you pour a bit of the sugar butter mixture into the eggs and whisk things a bit. Then add a bit more before pouring all the egg mixture into the saucepan. Just give everything a good stir. Then at the end you toss in two and a half cups of chopped pecans and a healthy slug of bourbon. Vanilla is expensive these days, and bourbon adds a nice smoky flavour to things. Yes, we are making do with bourbon like tragic fragile waifs selling matches on a street corner.

Once the crumb base is baked, you pour the pecan topping all over that and pop it back into the oven at 350°F/180°C for 30–40 minutes. It should be set when you remove it. It will need to cool for a couple of hours. Then you can cut it up into liberal slices, and snack on those while you make things and talk to each other late at night about your hopes, dreams and irritations. Even your cousin Jennifer who says, "I am going to be so bad and just have a tiny piece. I am going to have to work all of this off at the gym this weekend," will take a quarter of a slice and then slowly return for another quarter and another quarter. You don't judge her because you love her kind heart, the fact that she will always like your weird photos on Instagram, and that she will always stop what she is doing to help you get the perfect wings for your eyeliner. You eat these pecan bars with your mom, your grandma, your cousins, your sister, your Aunt Sharon who married your idiot Uncle Gary. ("God knows why she is still with him," you mutter to each other when she goes out to the car to bring in the relish tray.) Everyone else might hear cackles in the kitchen, but they won't know how much fun you are having.

ℰ

DEATH AT EVERY HOUR

Her eyelashes flicked against the pillow she was hugging. A polite and efficient knocking at the door, interspersed with the watery echo of muffled words from a bathroom, was insistent that her slumber was over—even if her headache wasn't. The itching, streaked remains of last night's make-up left her feeling like an iced cake left out too long after festivities. She tried to untangle herself from beaded necklaces and the disorientation of an unfamiliar room. A tail was draped over an elegant chair, next to a pair of cowboy boots and one of those movie-star ten-gallon hats. She was dressed as a mermaid, or had been. Where was this lone ranger?

The knock again. The door! She gathered up her sheets to fashion an improvised gown. The parched sea creature now looked as if she belonged to a godly temple in the sky after a run-in with Athena. Tumbling slightly from her lofty place when her bare foot encountered a forgotten toy pistol, she opened the door to a small, exquisitely uniformed man who offered a cordial greeting. "Good morning, Miss. Room service; may I enter?" The attendant paraded in with a covered trolley, quickly asking where she might like it. She pointed to the table that was crowded with a Leica camera, her evening bag, a travelling man's personal ephemera, and bottles from the night before. The placid man revealed to her what lay under the dome: toast, a small amount of butter, jam (not the usual rhubarb or glassy marmalade, she noted), eggs, champagne, ice, and an enormous pot of real coffee. As she signed the bill while holding tightly to the sheets that were beginning to fail as a covering, he focused on making sure the napkins were just so. The attendant was too well-trained and well-paid to offer visible judgement regarding the private lives of guests.

Once satisfied he said, "Thank you, Miss. If you require anything else, please do not hesitate to telephone. Good day." He withdrew and quietly closed the door.

An accented voice from the bath called out, "*Chéri*, did he bring extra coffee? I asked for extra coffee."

The cowboy!

She poured a cup for him and asked, "Cream? Sugar?"

"Black! I am not a child."

She adjusted her deconstructed dress as if preparing for a top of the act entrance and went into the bathroom. She found a hairy man with his legs draped over the side of the tub, reading a pulp novel. He accepted the coffee, which matched his hair: dark and glossy. Slapping a hand a bit too quickly to her face (thus causing her face to feel more than it was ready to at that painful hour), she exclaimed, "Oh bloody hell, I forgot to tip the man. He must think I have no idea how to behave. Please tip him extra after I leave."

"Leave? *Liebling*, we have to find you something more suitable than that swimming costume before we leave for Morocco."

"Morocco?"

"Yes. Sorted last night. Remember, after poker. I owe the artist a favour. You will help." He sipped his coffee and returned to his book.

"I don't think I am in the best position to skip off to Morocco. May I have breakfast first?"

"Why do you think I order eggs? Go eat. You had too much champagne last night. I have a cure for that. Be a good kitten and eat. Then I explain Morocco." He dismissed her like a child with a wave of his hand. She took the dressing gown hanging on the hook and left the sheet in its place. He smiled and said, "That was mine."

She replied, "You can get it back in Morocco."

Returning to breakfast laid out on the table, she saw that these were not the usual sharp-scented anaemic scrambled eggs concocted from the dry mix that all were supposed to be grateful for. These eggs had a brilliant dandelion-like hue and were just as puffed up as one in full bloom. Normally she would have a lack of enthusiasm at facing food after engaging in the decathlon of decadence, but these eggs gave off a soothing scent of butter and the promise of calming minor maladies. She poured herself some of her companion's coffee, adding plenty of milk and sugar because she didn't care if it made her a child. She had been many things and people over the last several hours, and while she was presently human, she wanted to shed the hangover that came with this mortal state. The first taste of eggs proved that they would abide by their covenant to heal. She asked, "Do you want me to save some of the eggs for you?"

"Eat, *liefde*. You need it. Bring coffee when you have finished."

Maybe the Morocco-bound man knew what was good for her.

She was pleased because she didn't want to share something so luxurious. He could have the hot water; she wanted hot eggs. And maybe toast too as it came with strawberry jam. The pleasures of hot buttered toast were always a present possibility; she was more concerned with the mystery of what had happened to her top. One of the clam shells had been lost during the destruction of the floats, but she knew she had worn something at the poker game. She hadn't played, so there was no literal shirt lost.

It didn't appear to be anywhere in the room. She finished her eggs, spread butter and the gem-toned jam on a piece of toast (she didn't believe in noble restraint when it came to toast) and poured more coffee. It was time to interview her only available witness. She returned to the bathroom. He had decided to return to his merman state; his legs were back in the bath, with more hot water being added. She handed him more coffee and he smiled and said, "*Danke*, sweet."

She sat down and asked, "Have you seen my top? Or the other clamshell?"

He laughed and said, "You must not remember. You offered your remaining clamshell to that one gentleman in need of an ashtray."

"Goodness. I hope he appreciated the gesture."

"He did buy everyone a round of drinks, and he thanked your sailor friend for catching such a clever mermaid in his net."

"I still had a top from my two-piece?"

"Remember when the artist hurt his hand on that bottle? You were quite the Florence Nightingale."

She remembered the artist cutting his hand and weeping about his career ending. She had whipped off the remains of her bikini top and provided a quick bandage.

She giggled and said, "Of course. I gave him a kiss on the head and told him that my training from the war ought to be good for something."

"He said he wants to paint you. Don't worry, love, someone lent you a scarf. You returned here civilised. Other than the tail and wearing my hat."

"No top. That makes it very difficult to travel to Tangiers."

"We will send for your things. You have a passport, yes?"

"Yes. I told you where I work. I couldn't have swum there."

"*Drágám*, yes, yes. How is your head? I believe it is time for a cure."

"What does my Hop-Along Casanova propose for a cure?"

"*Liefde*, bring the champagne and that other bottle on the table. The odd old one. And two glasses. Don't forget ice!"

She wondered if he would ever leave the bath. Would he shrink and swim away when the plug was let out? She brought him the necessary rations. He tossed the paperback onto the floor. Whilst remaining in his aquatic lounge, he began his demonstration.

"I learned about this drink from a true drunk. He claims to have invented it. Who knows? He invents sentences too. He is a bastard. Rogues know rogues. He would claim he could turn water into wine. Darling, hold the glasses."

She held them on the edge of the tub as instructed. He poured a liberal measure of sea-glass green liquid. "Absinthe!" he told her. "My friend the drunk always says to pour a jigger. Whatever that is. Pour enough."

He put the bottle on the floor and demanded, "Champagne now!" The bottle opened with ease. He snorted. "No need for swords or injured artists again." The champagne cascaded into the glasses, creating a froth that looked like foam on the beach before revealing contents that looked like a glimpse under the ocean as the sun came through. She was about to grab her drink when he said, "Not yet. Have you ever been to the Medina in Fez? I think you would find beauty there. Many colours. It is where they dye things. We could get you shoes. You will need them. Before you drink this, we must add ice. It will make the oils perform a magic trick. Watch." He dropped two ice cubes in and there was a sudden fog before her.

"Now you may drink. But slowly. We can't have you losing your tail as well."

"I lost that last night."

"Not the first time I hope."

She didn't answer as she was tasting this undeniably terrifying concoction that veered into medicinal territory before swinging away like an acrobat and landing in a net of pleasure and fizz. She wasn't quite sure if she liked it, but she felt the desire to take another sip before answering, "Oh goodness, no."

"The drink is that bad, pet?"

"No to my lost tail and yes to this. Though I am not sure if I should say yes to this."

"Smart girl. Just don't gulp it. I want to be able to return to this hotel. They are always so nice about the bills."

"I feel as if I am sitting by a roaring fire and I am a little too warm. Where was this when I was freezing during the war?" She leaned against the edge of the tub and stared at the milky bath. "You look like you are lying in the drink itself." She burst into giggles and took another sip that wasn't so slow. She felt herself veering between floating and sinking. Refocusing her vision to try and find a steady sense of gravity was a failure when concentrating on the mint-coloured tiles. It brought on a sinking sensation as if she was about to drown in the cocktail. Summoning the fragments of her sobriety to put together a coherent sentence, she said, "Do you mind terribly if I go and lie down? This is affecting my balance and I don't want to find myself swimming on the floor. Or waking in Morocco."

"I will wake you before we get on a plane. Go rest. We will sort out what you need for the trip."

She left him to his book and lethal prescription and sank back into bed. An evening that had begun at the arts students' ball with her friends the sailor, the lobster, and the starfish had led her to meet up again with the cowboy. She drank more of the cocktail and knew that this drink—like the man—was not a permanent fixture in her life but a damn fun brief adventure. Now to figure out how to plan her departure. When she had met him months ago in Berlin at that party, he had the good sense to be distracted with a decent hand at a poker game and she had a car waiting. She had also had clothes to leave in. It was time for a little assistance. She picked up the telephone and asked for a call to be put through to the one person who would ask questions but would also wait on judgement.

"Julia! Yes, I know I didn't come home last night ... No ... Can you leave for a bit and bring me a dress, and knickers ... Because I can't go on the Tube as a topless mermaid ... Well, I am not at my most sober and I don't want to end up in the papers ... Yes. No, not him. Ha! I will tell you when I am decent ... No, I don't need bus fare."

She gave her sister the address and hung up. She began to gather up the remains of her previous identity and put them with her handbag. Her Neptunian barman showed no sign of exiting his bath and all she had to do was wait and enjoy her drink. The knock eventually arrived and with it her sister, who provided the means of escape and an amused expression. "Well, Mata Hari," she asked, "where shall we take you?"

"Hush. To bed, if I am honest."

"What's wrong with that one over there?"

Giving Julia a look, she quickly slipped out of the robe, pulled on a dress, and yanked up her knickers. "Of course you brought the ones that aren't comfortable."

"You didn't put in a specific request. I just pulled those off the line. Next time keep a set with you."

"Shhhh. He will hear you."

The man from the bath asked, "Is that room service? Did you order more coffee? Mine is cold."

She called out, "No, I needed something else. But I can order you more coffee."

"You are a darling, *fleur*."

She pointed to the phone and asked her sister to telephone, while stuffing her mermaid remains into the bag. She went into the bathroom and got down on her knees and kissed him on the ear. He didn't bother looking away from his book as he said, "I have always liked the room service here."

Playing with his hair she said, "Bandi, I must fly."

"To Casablanca, yes?"

"One day. By the way, my name is Violet. Hopefully you can remember it, should you find me in Rome this spring."

"I could never forget my *fleur*."

"Tell your friend the drunk that his cocktail almost tempted me to Morocco. If I had had a second one, I would have gone in just my tail and beads."

"It's never too late."

"Let's have that next drink in Rome."

She kissed him goodbye and left him to soak for another hour with his stories of lurid French crime.

She found Julia eating a slice of cold toast with jam. She defended this action with the comment, "It wasn't rhubarb, and of course I am going to eat it. Can we take the champagne too?"

Violet picked up the spare bottle as fair payment for her sister's kindness. They left as the attendant was returning with more coffee for her gentleman friend. She told the man, "I owe you for earlier, chap." She gave him a few shillings and added, "The best eggs ever."

Violet and Julia got into the lift. Julia, taking possession of the champagne proudly in one hand, pulled out from her coat pocket a toy pistol from the cowboy's costume and said, "Who should we rob next?"

℃

JUST ONE, SINCE YOU ARE OFFERING

As Betty Draper would say, "My People are Nordic." Therefore I appreciate a good bar cookie. It goes well with a nice cup of coffee and a little commentary about how this isn't too bad a deal. If the bar cookie is especially good you might say, "You could do a lot worse." Ross cookies are rather popular in my family. They don't require a great deal of effort and have a sort of pleasing simplicity. (After all, brown sugar and butter are involved.)

You will cream together eight ounces of butter with a cup of firmly packed brown sugar. You may find this decadent, but sometimes you must sacrifice a few years of your life for the good of butter. You will mix in one egg yolk (save the egg white in the freezer so that you will eventually have enough to make angel food cake. One must have cake) and a tablespoon of vanilla extract. Have a taste. One has to make sure the butter and sugar and everything tastes good. I like to think of it as offering it up by taking the time to potentially risk a little food poisoning, tasting the cookie dough. Then mix in two cups of flour. It will be a fairly stiff dough. You will spread the dough out in a lightly buttered 9"x11" inch pan or jelly roll pan. Press it down evenly with your hands. Bake that at 350°F/180°C for about 15–20 minutes.

While that is baking you will start in on your fifth cup of coffee that day and get out a bar of chocolate. If you are a bittersweet sort of person you can use that. I suggest using semi-sweet. What sort of chocolate is really up to your palate. You will chop it up into little tiny pieces. When the cookie is done baking you will remove it from the oven (obviously; it isn't like you are going to send the cookie to Timbuktu) and spread the chocolate bits all over the base, leaving a quarter inch border. Just let the chocolate bits soften and melt. Maybe have another cup of coffee while this is going on, and maybe a short conversation about the Minnesota Twins' chances this year, or how Cousin Ruth shared this recipe for Snickers bar salad and how you thought, "That was *different*." (Seriously, this conversation once happened in my family, and that salad recipe exists.) Once the chocolate has melted, just take a palette knife (or just a regular butter knife; not everyone collects pastry-related knives like they are commemorative spoons) and spread that chocolate around (again, making sure you have that border). Oh, how delicious this will be. Then finely chop about a cup of nuts. Pecan or walnut is preferred. (One time I used pistachio. It was pretty decadent.) You will sprinkle that over the chocolate.

Then let everything cool for about half an hour. (This will allow you some time to talk about how the Sons of Norway are having a lutefisk feed. You may go, but they better have enough butter for the lutefisk because otherwise you won't be able to eat the stuff.) Then cut the Ross cookies into squares. If you have some willpower (though if you like to taste creamed butter and sugar I doubt you are the sort of person to wait) you will wait until the cookies have completely cooled and then eat them up. You can bring them to coffee hour at church, potluck night at the Grange, or the book club that is really the sipping-wine-and-talking-about-The-Crown club.

ℰ

WITH GREAT RAGE:
HOW TO SORTA COOK A POT ROAST

WHY IS EVERYONE BEING SO AWFUL AND ANNOYING AND *THERE* TODAY???? I want to throw plates, and shove a few people, and I dunno ... eat a pot roast. Why don't I have pot roast more often? We are going to eat pot roast so I don't punch some of you for having fool ass opinions and doing dumb things that I have to look at. Also I have the ingredients to make pot roast and maybe you do too. Let's make pot roast.

The first step is to inhale a bag of maple bacon crisps because the bag is open and you should get rid of them before someone else eats them. Someone who doesn't deserve them. Also, after looking in the fridge, I realize we don't have everything for the pot roast—namely the thing we are going to roast. So first let's go to the grocery store and side eye everyone in the aisles. Do those two guys have to have their super important conversation right by the meat case about what Kev did at the pub the other night? Do they realize how much space they are taking? You take up too much space. Make yourselves smaller. Much smaller. Lower. Yes, like that. Now talk in a quiet voice. Shhhh, much quieter. Now leave. Never come back.

Let's look at the cuts of meat. There is the deluxe meat, which is so tender that it drinks Earl Grey tea and is still not over the death of a parakeet five years ago. Ignore that meat. That meat is for another day. You need a chuck roast, a brisket. Something that has been around a while, hasn't experienced a massage, and knows what it is about. "Please cook me down in liquid at a low heat for many hours and I will make you feel okay about stuff." Put that in your basket. Along with some onions because you know you probably don't have any onions at home, because you used them up and forgot about that. Onions are ignored like the fifth child in a family of eight. "Where's Steve? He was around a bit ago." "He moved out of the house three years ago, MOM."

You may also buy yourself some peanut butter cups and eat those in the car while sitting in the parking lot. Maybe listen to a program on the radio about the 1930s Federal Theatre project and think to yourself, "Where is everyone's interest in the arts???" You angrily eat that second peanut butter cup and go home. You find one of the cats has thrown up on the floor because they ate their food too quickly. You swear for a couple of seconds, take a deep breath, clean it up and remind the cat, "You have lived with us for THREE YEARS. We will always feed you. You act like you lived in a refugee camp for several years fighting everyone for a cup of rice. COOL IT!!!"

Now let's get to work. (Also wash your hands after dealing with the cat.)

This pot roast is going to be done in the oven. My life is always a bit disorganized and I still don't own a crockpot. Yet I own escargot plates. Nothing about life makes sense, does it?

Pat your hunk of meat dry with some paper towels. Then coat with flour and a bit of salt and pepper. Nothing else. Nooo, you don't need some mushroom paste, or anything that sounds like a chic coconut-based moisturizer that will provide the meat with small pores and extra flavour.

Heat up your pot over high heat, add some fat (it should sizzle) and then sear that meat on all sides so it is brown, forms a nice crust and smoke starts filling the room and you remember to turn on the fan and open the windows and damn, maybe the heat is a bit too high so turn it down a bit. Remove the meat from the heat, plop it on a plate and then add some chopped up onions to the pot and cook them a bit. Add some smashed garlic. How many cloves? More than a WASP would put in. So at least two. More like four because you are there and you might as well add more garlic. Toss in some thyme, and a bit of marjoram because it is fun to say marjoram. And if someone asks, "Is this oregano?" you can say, "NOPE!" and then stuff another potato in your mouth before you get even more annoyed with them. (Listen, Dave, there isn't some kind of prize for knowing the herbs in a dish. JUST EAT THE MEAL AND LEAVE ME IN PEACE.) Don't forget to add some tomato paste. Toss things around like you know what you are doing—even though you really don't. "I am making up everything as I go along. Christ ... John Goodman's character in 'Matinee' was totally right. I could be a circus star or an assassin and no one would really know."

You are distracted and things are smelling smoky again. DAMMIT. So you add some beef stock (use a cube and hot water for all I care. It works. Most people do and life goes on. IT GOES ON!) and some red wine. Why not use that goth-looking wine from Hungary you bought because the label looked cool. It just needs to be okay and not taste like really awful vinegar. I suppose this Goth wine tastes sort of chocolatey. I have no idea about wine. WHO CARES! Pour it all in, deglaze the pan. (Scrape up the bits because you left it too long while you considered who annoys you today.) Then add the meat to everything. It isn't going to climb in there like Bugs Bunny taking a bath. You have to make the effort here.

Let it simmer and then cover with a lid and pop it into the oven at 325°F/160°C for a couple of hours. In the meanwhile, you need to remind yourself to avoid certain elements of social media so you don't accidentally get all real on people and maybe burn a couple of bridges or five because everyone is just so short-sighted and OMG ... they just HAD to post that didn't they??? WHY did we look? We should unfollow everyone so we will still like them. Or at least do a better job of pretending. Spend the next couple of hours doing some angry vacuuming, maybe a bit of spiteful scrubbing of the bathtub (working on several imaginary arguments while you make things gleam), and maybe watching a Netflix documentary about cats or wine country. Something that keeps you from seething about something. Maybe Hitler documentaries calm you down. Whatever works.

It is time to return to that pot roast. The meat should be fairly tender but not tender enough that it feels vulnerable and safe to give up its secrets about its life, and what truly makes it cry. The meat should merely admit, "It hasn't been easy, but this bath of wine and stock sure feels good." Toss in some root vegetables. You know what you like and what you have in the kitchen. Just make sure things are cut fairly thick. You want the vegetables soft in the end but not like baby food. And no celery. Do you WANT TO RUIN DINNER?! I mean, sure, fine, go ahead, it's your dinner, but don't hate yourself and everyone around you! Give it another hour and a half. Keep that heat low, maybe drop it a bit further.

Once it appears done, the meat should practically fall apart and admit that it doesn't really think it knows what love is and always walks away before things get too real and it just wants someone to feel that they are the best. It is tired of being all strong and acting like Kelly and choosing themselves. It wants someone to choose them. Yeah, you are having that kind of a meal. Move the vegetables and meat to a large dish and take the liquid and maybe thicken it a bit. I am a fan of mixing butter and flour together and then slowly dropping it into the liquid while whisking over medium heat. Give everything a bit of a taste. Maybe the gravy needs a touch of salt and pepper—likely not, but you know what you like. Add everything back together and serve it up.

By this point in the day you are exhausted and kind of hungry. You had too many cups of tea or coffee and probably not enough protein, or a nap. You really should work on that a bit. Yes, the world can be sort of horrible some days, and yeah, people can act a little foolish, but we are all just trying. Well okay ... some are trying. Some are just lazy idiots or truly selfish creeps. But plenty of people are kind, compassionate, and want to do right. Remember that. Eat the pot roast and feel a little better. Save room for dessert. (Because you forgot you bought a chocolate bar a while ago and hey, surprise, chocolate.)

ℰ

ANOTHER BROWNIE RECIPE
FOR THE UNSATISFIED

Mrs H., a wise family friend, once said of raising children (and she raised many), "There is always one that humbles you." You want to feed that child of yours. You know how to cook and bake and make beautiful things, but they look upon everything with disinterest at best and disgust at worst. You keep trying and trying. You are a magician on stage trying to find that one trick that delights your demanding audience. Some days you sigh and mutter, "Fine, have another feckin' Jaffa cake ... " But you keep trying as you want that person to taste your love. You want them to have their eyes light up. You think you have narrowed down all of their criticisms and will make something that will surprise them. It probably won't happen today but that is okay.

These aren't squidgy, dense, or packed full of hashish à la Alice B. Toklas. They are a simple cake-like brownie. Not too moist, but they hold up pretty well. Let's begin our masochistic ritual. You know the drill. You have been here before. Preheat the oven to 350°F/180°C and butter and flour an 8"x8" pan. You can probably do this in your sleep. Melt down three ounces of chocolate and set aside. Cream together two ounces of butter and seven ounces of white sugar (that's right, we aren't shy about sugar. You want to make those taste buds come to life). Then add two eggs. Yes, there is less butter, but you will get moisture and fats elsewhere. Have a little faith. Just like the faith you have that one day your child will eat a vegetable, or hopefully won't get scurvy from not touching a single one for three years running. Then add three tablespoons of milk, one teaspoon of vanilla extract, and the melted chocolate. It will be a light milky chocolate colour. In another bowl (yeah, it is one of those brownie recipes that wants you to dirty a few dishes. Make someone else do the washing up), sift together two and a half ounces of flour, half a teaspoon of baking powder, and a dash of salt. Add that to the batter and mix until the white streaks disappear. Pour that into your pan and bake for about 25–30 minutes. (You know how your oven behaves, adjust accordingly.)

While that bakes, you can remind yourself that most children grow out of this and won't live on a diet of raspberries, cheese sticks, and sausage rolls when they are an adult. And if they do, it isn't your problem anymore. You briefly consider those recipes where one sneaks spinach into a brownie recipe but you know that your darling child will immediately spot the flavour and not touch them and then *you* have to eat the wretched things. So don't put yourself through that personal hell.

Remove the brownies from the oven, let them cool, and then offer one to the child with a strong will and firm opinions. The things that will make them a fantastic adult are sometimes the things that help you find all kinds of patience, love and new brownie recipes. And if they don't like the brownie, I am sure someone else will. Just hand the kid another Jaffa cake and give them a hug.

ℰ

SWEETBREADS AND SCAMS

Abstruse bon vivant looking to find a willing soul who wants to explore the pleasures of the demi-monde. Be it over sweetbreads, my record collection, or absinthe; we choose to be unbound by any traditions. Let's engage in rites of our own making.

"You sound like Maurice Chevalier. Will you dance me around the room? I must confess, there might be a bit of competition, as sweetbreads have my heart."

"Girls like you shouldn't exist. To love sweetbreads is to understand our innate carnality as humans. Maybe the sweetbreads can be a third."

❧

Alastair was forty. Allegedly. He put forty on his profile because, as he often told the girls who made his espresso at his local coffee shop, he didn't feel fifty-three. It wasn't like he was applying for a credit card and needed to be specific about his personal details. He was still looking for a beautiful creature who wanted to embrace his gifts of experience and taste. Today, modern technology presented him with Selene. She was so new to adulthood (barely twenty) that he could feel her wanting to impress him via her texts. He would make sure to explain that her vitality was enough for him. He decided to skip the coffee date he required of most women. He had rules about not going to dinner with someone who had syrups in their coffee drinks; unless they were especially pretty like that lithe ballerina he spent a few months with before she left suddenly for a ballet company in Denmark. As he told his newest therapist, "It was never meant to be; she only read books published in this century."

Selene was different. He insisted they have dinner that very night and she agreed. There would be sweetbreads.

"They aren't as good as this one place I used to go, but they are a suitable introduction for your tender tongue."

"That is a pretty big promise. I can't wait to try them."

He offered to pick her up. She suggested that they should meet somewhere significant and then walk together. He liked her cinematic ideas. They met in front of an old clock that had forgotten how to tell time. Alastair appeared in what he felt was his best rakish uniform. An old suit of good quality and interesting history. No tie, for this was a city that didn't appreciate his sartorial originality. Instead he sported a scarf that allowed him to tell a story about being in Italy and meeting Graham Greene.

Selene appeared as if carried by the wind. She removed a clip from the back of her head and shook her dark blonde hair free from its contained state. Alastair thought she looked a bit like Françoise Hardy, the way her fringe fell into her eyes and her hair looked so casual. He doubted she would know of the singer if he made such a reference. He smiled and thought, *one more thing to educate her about.* Selene was all in black, from her simple jersey dress to her cardigan decorated with a few sequins near the neck. The mary janes on her feet seemed more appropriate for school. She was shorter than he had imagined. She still had the full cheeks of recent adolescence. She smiled and said, "Excuse my dress—I just came from work. I should either be serving coffee or working in a funeral home."

"Which is it, darling?"
"The one that tips better."

⌘

Alastair had an imp on his hands. He could not be more excited. She could be like a puppy who nips to play. At dinner he was captivated with how she asked him questions. He got to tell her his favourite stories and explain to her about each dish. She complimented his suit, and he handled the lapel with love and said, "It is vintage Hugo Boss. Before they were branded in the 70s. Something a bit special."

Selene began to play with her fork on the table and asked, "Didn't Hugo Boss design uniforms for the Nazis?"

Alastair was taken aback. It felt like an accusation. He smiled with his teeth and told her, "I suppose so. But this was made after that unpleasantness. Also, you shouldn't play with your fork."

Selene smiled, but not with her teeth, and said, "Of course. You do wear it well. The suit I mean."

That small compliment made him think she was going to be open to so many things.

He was amused when she took out a small green notebook and a nubby pencil and wrote down things he told her. She was hungry not only for dinner but his opinions. She was enthusiastic about the sweetbreads and told him he was right and encouraged him to pick other dishes for them to try. He ordered more wine. It was over the fourth glass of a white burgundy (which Alistair had chosen because he said the first mistake everyone makes is to pair red with such a tender meat, and he would never be able to look himself in the mirror if he had chosen some pinot noir) that he said, "You would make a great protégée like Jane Birkin."

"Not France Gall?"

"Pardon?"

"More bread?"

"Only if you have more wine."

Selene held out her glass and laughed but he failed to notice that she barely touched the drink. He decided that he was going to make her his favourite cocktail (a Gibson—always with Spanish onions) back at his place. Once the bill was paid, Alastair looked at her and said, "You have passed the first test. Let's go celebrate."

Selene dramatically pushed her fringe to one side as if to rest from great labour and said, "Have I now? Lucky me."

Alistair leaned forward and brushed the fringe back so it nearly covered her eyes. He spoke more to himself when he said, "Yes, very much Jane Birkin."

Selene looked away, which Alistair took as sudden shyness. He loved it.

They stood up to leave, and she pulled something out of her handbag and slipped it into her pocket and asked him with a detached cheeriness, "Ready to go?"

❧

He walked her out with his hand initially on the small of her back before it slid over to her waist and he could pull her a little closer. He thought her perfume was a touch juvenile—always vanilla with girls that age. He would have to introduce her to something more refined or exotic. Maybe a gift if he was feeling generous. Alistair knew he would have some stories for his old buddy Ed when they got together for their weekly drinks at the bar.

Alastair and Selene stood outside of the restaurant. He put both hands around her waist and told her, "I think it is time we have you on my sofa."

She laughed and said, "I am far too full to consider dessert."

Before Alastair could say dessert wasn't on offer, Selene gave him a peck on the cheek and ran to the corner and leapt onto the waiting bus like she was another dancer needing to make a quick exit.

For the first time that evening Alastair couldn't put words together.

Selene, on the other hand, swiped her bus card and found a seat next to a sleeping nurse. She began quickly writing down more words in her notebook. She found the act of physically writing down words helped her recall every element of dinner.

"Sweetbreads, grilled, with lemon. The flavour was gentler than I had anticipated. To some, offal tastes musty. This was full of life and was a lot more interesting than my dining companion." She crossed out that line because he wasn't that dull—he was absolutely silly. He had told her about his two ex-wives before they finished the first course of anchovies and croquettes. She was more interested in how the garlic and cayenne pepper added more to the fish than his explanation as to why he ended his first marriage. She knew she would have to call the restaurant to ask a bunch of questions.

He told her twice that he liked her youth because she wasn't bitter about love or life like his second wife Amanda had been. Over the tripotx (a kind of lamb's blood sausage that she had never encountered before), Selene asked him about his scarf to be polite, as he kept touching it and arranging it. He took a bite of the sausage and related a long story about where he had purchased it in a place where he had actually given Graham Greene writing advice. Alastair tossed off a few book titles that he said she needed to check out. She let him continue to talk so that she could concentrate upon the food. Selene was going to write a heck of an article for the website. Maybe one day she could thank Alastair for being a part of her writing journey—if she ever got paid. But first she wanted to perfect this sentence. She just wished she had ordered dessert—the *pastel Vasco* looked so pleasing.

She had emailed her editor telling him that she was going to review this place, and he said that if she did a good job that they might promote it a bit more. No money. Just exposure. Even though she was getting good numbers for the reviews. When she was invited to contribute to the site everyone told her it was a great opportunity. No, they wouldn't cover the cost of meals, but if she was a bit short of money couldn't she ask her parents to help her financially? She wasn't sure how to explain real life to this crowd of men in hoodies and poorly fitted jeans, who viewed public transportation as a novelty at 2am.

She knew some would call her mercenary in how she chose to solve her problem. Her roommate Meg thought Selene was playing a dangerous game. Selene said to her one night over beer and cheap pho, "They made the game. They just don't like it when you read the full rules and discover the loopholes."

Selene was learning so much about the world in this adventure. She discovered which restaurants (like some of her dates) were riding high on an ancient reputation. It was at the Four Seasons where she had the lousiest steak she had ever eaten in her life. She let the world know it too. She loved talking to chefs and everyone back of house about their work. That is where the real circus was happening, and she wanted to introduce people to that. As the bus took her home, she continued to write down her recollections. Then a notification on her phone. Another ad answered. An interest in dinner. *Vietnamese perhaps?* Selene smiled and texted her editor with another pitch.

PLATEFUL OF PAIN AND LOVE

My father once tried to strangle me over marinara. He was angry that I slammed the door of his car, but the real source of his rage was that I told him his plans for dinner weren't good because his spaghetti sauce was terrible and none of my siblings were going to like it. I was right. Bad marinara isn't a crime against humanity, but it should be worth a night or two in the county jail.

My mother and father met in a restaurant. My mother was captivated as he was very tall, with fashionably long pretty dark hair in ringlets, and sharp cheekbones. He had an easy charisma that immediately drew my mother in. When they eventually went out on a proper date (my mother said that technically their first date was at a Native American biker bar where a knife fight broke out, but I think napkins need to be involved for it to be real to her), they went to a Chinese barbecue joint where my mother faced a menu that was mostly in Cantonese, and parts of animals she had never eaten. My father was testing her to see if she was cool enough to hang. My mother hung on with her fearless love for over twenty years.

In the end she found the Chinese barbecue joint was a more reliable bet.

There were always tests. When I was six years old, he put me in front of a bunch of rowdy Australian sailors who balked at the idea of eating raw oysters at the restaurant where he was chef. He wanted to show them how cool he was to have a daughter who ate oysters and how small they were to be afraid. He was fortunate to have a daughter who liked oysters, and who loved him very much. I always kept hoping that I would be given a taste of the pride he gobbled up for himself. He liked liverwurst, so I ate liverwurst. I wouldn't eat my mother's pork fried rice, but I would eat his Hoppin' John. He would make strange intense heat-filled dishes filled with offal. I would eat it up even as it hurt me, and ask for seconds.

I think of his knife-scarred chef's hands moving quickly in the kitchen as he would make me porridge, or hash browns for breakfast. If you were worthy, he could be very charming and generous with his gifts and knowledge. He introduced my mother to different cuisines and taught her a few things. Then she made the unspoken mistake of being talented and surpassing his skills. He kept finding ways to punish her for his pain and insecurity. He preferred to be that bright star and didn't care how steadfast some were in their affection. Then came the day I saw how dull his light was. I wanted nothing to do with it because I saw how it distorted everything—or, when his ire was great, it caused things to wither. I was filled with rage as I witnessed how he tried to steal my mother's spirit and was beginning to test and take from my siblings too. I had to push him out of the kitchen.

I am descended from two islands in Europe. My mother's people came from an island in the north, and my father's came from an island in the south. They are two islands with a dedication to feuding and grudge-holding. Both have a history of being repeatedly invaded and often co-opting their invaders' cultures. (The enthusiasm varies.) They are people who have always eaten and lived in defiance of those who wish to oppress them. The women in both places are known for possessing a great steeliness that has always been tied to the adoration of goddesses and early saints. Tales of fortitude, miracles and revenge are passed down so that every girl knows how to keep living even if they must carry their suffering with them. I have my father's chin, and his nose.

From my mother I have her large and always knowing eyes, and her frustrating, unyielding nature. My father never had a chance with women like that in the house. My mother didn't know she had given birth to this accidental witch with twice the strength from her ancestors because my father had hidden so much of his true self. The only thing my mother knew was that her first born was incredibly obstinate, and that each child who came after possessed the same wild nature. She loved each of us and brought us into the kitchen in our individual ways. Her great pride is that in the company of her children she and others are always well fed.

It was halfway through my childhood (as my own gifts in the kitchen were forming) that my father's true identity came to the surface. One would have thought that to be unburdened from so many secrets would have released him from his anger. All it did was make him more cruel. With it began the hostilities between him and me. My response was to take dinner from him. Then I took Thanksgiving. When my mother wasn't well, I took over Christmas dinner. I was gathering the love and adoration he sought. He expected it to be given to him as if it were his birth right. He made attempts to claim credit for my abilities, and his lies were exposed by my mother, and me. Sometimes a simple "No you didn't" would interrupt his posturing. Still, I had to be careful. He would find new ways to strike at any moment and sabotage things. He truly believed he was the creator of everything in his midst and that he had a right to destroy what he liked. It went hand in hand with his tirades about his expectations of respect. But the bitter sorcerer was losing.

Then came the day my mother found her strength. She told people she was going on a vision quest. Where I grew up you can tell people that and they will nod with understanding. (I come from a town where people regularly speak to ghosts, so reality is a more varied experience.) She had to travel to Montana to retrieve a part of herself. As a child she had visited a spot where a great battle had taken place. The indigenous people of the plains had been fighting to prevent their sacred lands from being taken from them, and the battle of the greasy grass was a powerful victory for them. It was the one where they struck down a tyrant. (The defeat had been foretold at the Sun Dance ceremony by Tȟatȟáŋka Íyotake.) She arrived on the anniversary, and it was like drinking from a well that reminded her of her tenacity. She came home and knew my father had to leave. As their division was becoming complete, his last act with me was over that marinara sauce. That same night I encountered him in the car park of a grocery store. (My mother and I were on our way to buy ice cream to numb the day.) I wasn't going to sup on anger. I began to roar, all the air ashake. His pride was poisonous and I wanted no more. I declared that as my father he was dead to me. I turned him into a phantom.

❦

What do you do once you rid the house of a bad spirit? You make a soufflé. You order Chinese take-away for Easter dinner. You eat great quantities of cinnamon toast at odd hours while watching old films. In the early days of freedom we had what a friend called an emotional rumspringa. This extra space in our lives had to be filled. I went to markets. I touched everything. I made bread at strange hours. I wrote down what I made, while my mother nudged more cookbooks and recipes in my direction.

"You should make this."

"I wonder what that would taste like."

My two youngest siblings would argue about what I was to make for dessert. They were the only children in existence who would complain about a soufflé or madeleines being made. Again. My brother Tom was at a stage of adolescence where his main occupation was eating. My efforts had somewhere to go no matter how they turned out. Whether it was three pm or three am, he always seemed to have a plate in hand.

I was an adult who came and went, but I kept returning to my mother's house to cook. Maybe I had to keep cooking to make sure he didn't return. I wasn't a witch who had complete confidence in my spells.

My family began to refer to my father as the Late Mr. G. Any queries about his mortal state were quickly explained away with the comment, "He is not dead. We just felt he had to go." It was our way of handling the inevitable uncomfortable questions about his lack of presence in our lives, and long-held-back thoughts about his general personality. (Divorce, or death, seems to loosen people's tongues so that tact is an afterthought.)

I may have banished him, but he was a spectre who refused to stay in the netherworld. I wanted nothing to do with him. First, he was the villain who I made a point to be nothing like. Every single part of him was seen as tainted. As I became more zealous in the kitchen, there were certain dishes I did not even look at for years, as they were corrupted by association. I went from a life of tacos, tamales, spaghetti, and clams to touching tacos maybe five times in my entire twenties. It was a decade when I abstained, but not so courteously. Then I had children and I saw him as a bewildering tragedy. I found myself recalling moments in the kitchen with him as I fed my own children. I kept wondering why he hadn't been able to love freely the way I found myself loving my children as I made dinner and watched them discover what they liked and didn't like at the table. From my mother I learned patience and keeping a sense of humour about trying to feed children. I have one child who will eat nearly everything, and one who has very definite opinions about what they want to eat. My mother said of one of my siblings, "When it came to dinner, for about three years they lived on air, and the occasional serving of fried chicken." She didn't shut off her love, she merely kept showing us what the cupboards and fridge could offer.

I moved far away to the island of my husband's people and found myself craving the things I had kept away from myself and my family. I had to go to great lengths to find certain ingredients, but it was good to learn that tamales or provolone could not cause an epidemic of emotional pain in others. Cooking foods from home and my childhood was one of my few sources of comfort because I found myself feeling very lonely on this island. The language was mostly familiar, the culture I sort of knew, but every single day was a challenge. There was always a reminder that I was an outsider and that while it was where I lived, it wasn't home.

I would eat the food of the island and everything tasted off. Cakes felt dry in my mouth, the bacon wasn't crisp, peaches and nectarines weren't sweet, and risotto was too crowded and never creamy enough. I felt like I could only trust my own hands in the kitchen to feed me well. I carried my own mark of pain. It was much like my birthmark that is hidden and only visible to a few. The melancholy was mine own. The darkness came to slowly freeze my soul. I found myself drifting away from the world. Then food stopped grounding me. I was hungry for something, but I had no idea what, and that appetite for living began to grow smaller.

When that windy cliff-edge twilight begins to take over the landscape, the approaching endless night becomes still and wants to tell its version of the story of you. It decides what you are worthy of loving and what you want to feast upon. Usually it says you don't get to have anything. That you don't deserve any of that. Day after day. Stuck. Nor breath or motion to excite me. I didn't have good spirits to guide me out. I found myself brandishing some of the same tendencies as my father: displaying a brittle, arrogant tone when others attempted to show their concern for me. I wanted to be a comet that would disappear before anyone could see what I saw as the horror that resided within me. I tried to hide it from myself and others.

My mother came to visit. She could see some of it within me. We went to Ireland, where her people had come from. It is a land of storytellers, and she told stories as we drove everywhere. She told me stories of her life, and of others. We saw the lines in the hillsides where potatoes once grew and fed so many before they had to escape starvation. We drank tea and I told her how in the nineteenth century the British thought the Irish feckless and decadent for spending money on good strong tea. The people of Connemara became known for putting plenty of sugar in their tea while they took their time to enjoy every single sip. We learned that this was the land where they didn't hold back with butter. There were plenty of ways that they were told they were sinners but, by God or Anu, they weren't going to have the pleasure of bread and butter and tea taken from them. She told me about her defiant family who did things their own way. My mother fed me hope and reminded me of my own nature. The little girl who would pick every single piece of raw onion out of her food, and the woman who while in active labour picked blackberries and made a crumble for her family. I thought I had as much value as a dog pancake. I was a blight, and the worst part was to find myself knowing this shadow of a man and why he did everything. I was beginning to wonder: if one cut me open like a lemon, might they find something rotten in the centre?

❦

The Akan people who reside around what was once known as the Gold Coast of West Africa (now modern-day Ghana) have this philosophy of personhood that consists of five parts: the body (Nipadua), the soul (Okra), the spirit (Sunsum), the character from the father, and the character from the mother. It is a matrilineal culture, so the mother's contribution (Mogya) is the blood/identity while the father's (Ntoro) is about the inheritance of his spiritual and characteristic traits. I don't know how many parts I have to my personhood, but my spirit took me one early spring day to Sicily: the island of my father's people. As I stood on the tarmac I stared at Mount Etna. It was like being greeted by a distant cousin or an auntie who didn't want me to miss her in the crowd. I grew up with the shifting nature of volcanoes. Some fear volcanoes, thinking of them as capricious, but if you live with one long enough, you know their eruptions don't come out of nothing. What many don't realise is that their outbursts also provide great gifts like the rich soil. The Trinacria is the symbol of the island. Extending from the head of the Gorgon (daughters of the sea Gods) are ears of wheat to represent Sicily's fertility, as it was known as the breadbasket of ancient Rome.

This is a place that has always fed people. Everywhere I went my stomach and soul were fed. When I arrived in Catania, I adopted my preferred persona of *la flâneuse*. Within seconds of leaving the flat I was surrounded by offerings of food. It wasn't asked outright, but I could sense that familial question, "Have you eaten?" I walked into the night and took in the scent of the orange trees that were along the streets, felt my child-like draw to the colours and bright lights of gelaterias, and then played my favourite game of not having plans and letting myself be fed by whim.

I landed in a restaurant that was filled with locals and a man singing standards from the 1950s and '60s. There were children eating with their parents late into the night. As I ate the marinated seafood, fried anchovies and mussels with pasta, I recalled being with my brother, my mother and her friends at the local Italian restaurant on Saturday nights. Jazz would be playing and my brother and I would grow bored waiting for pizza or pasta. We would play on the front steps of the restaurant (often running into a brother and sister we were friends with, as their father's art studio was next door, and their mother was sometimes cooking in the restaurant). In the restaurant I watched as a chef came out to greet his family, who had come for a late meal. I could see a conversation I witnessed many times over: a tired mother recounting her day while holding a wiggling child who wasn't so interested in dinner, while the other child was doodling and interrupting with questions. The chef half-listened before returning to the line.

✍

On my return from a long afternoon walk, I watched the growing queue at a stall that sold *crespelle di riso*: sweet, crispy rice fritters, often produced for the festival of Saint Joseph in March. (Which toppings are offered will tell you where you are: sugar in Messina, sour cherries in Syracuse, and honey in Catania). I picked a few different things and the man handed me one that was thick with honey and told me to eat while they prepared my order. My openly displayed bliss made the other men behind the counter laugh.

Every single time I looked at food and ate, I had the smile of a child. It was Christmas to be handed a cone of fried calamari, or to find lovingly displayed produce. All over Catania there was something that would delight me. From the people on the street selling spleen sandwiches against the backdrop of graffiti criticizing Salvini and fascism, to the woman with a small art studio who was fervent about her city and island with its rough reputation. Via traditional arts she wanted others to see the resilience of the people and the culture. I noticed the image of Saint Agatha (the patron saint of Catania), and the artist spoke of the saint's strength being a source of inspiration. (Agatha was tortured in a million different ways but was unwavering in her identity.)

Agatha is so venerated that she was named the patroness for all of Sicily. She followed me all over the island in shrines vast and small. Everywhere I was met with symbols of courage. In the Nebrodi mountains I encountered wild boars on the road. In a moment of my own wildness I got out of the car and stood to watch a Nebrodi sow and her piglets. A Latin friend of mine likes to say that magical realism is realism where he comes from. When I told him about meeting the animals on the edge of the woods, he said the wild pigs were sent to me as a gift: to the Celts they are symbols of fearlessness. The wild pigs also represent stubbornness and chaos. Those two are the salt and pepper that have seasoned much of my life.

❦

The Akan people believe that the okra (soul) is the life force given to each being. They will speak of someone having a happy, disturbed or sad okra. The attributes of the Sunsum (spirit) are made up of our characteristics, and there is a belief that the choices a person makes with their spirit can affect the state of the soul. The Akan have a deep sense of their ties to community and yet they have this proverb: *The clan is like a cluster of trees which, when seen from afar, appeared huddled together, but which would be seen to stand individually when closely approached.* There is recognition of what the individual can bring to the community, and what the community brings to the individual. There might be conflict, but there is always the possibility of finding a way to integrate the experience and value of each person into the collective noise.

In Palermo I found the secret rhythm in chaos. It is like picking up the humming in Glenn Gould's recordings and knowing it adds a layer of intimate richness to the experience. From the way people drove and honked their horns (which served a true purpose: to alert each other in a sly and practical way) to ease of faith I found in following the adventure and taking people as they were.

One night there was a meal that was practically a history lesson on the plate of everyone who had dominated (as the Sicilians say) the people. Tunisian brik, as the island was part of a few Arabic caliphates; *farsumagru* from the Normans (who embraced many Arabic dishes within the cuisine); pumpkin in a risotto from the New World (the age of exploration brought Spanish nobility to the island, and those Bourbons brought a grandness in the approach to eating). That was the restaurant where everyone was from everywhere. The server's family came from Morocco, and half the kitchen staff came from Sudan or Eritrea. I could hear French and Spanish being spoken at one table, and then the Sicilian dialect. There is always room at the table for one more dish, or guest, because there might be something good.

I kept finding something good everywhere I wandered. There was the grandmother I spoke to who had her disabled grandson with her. He wasn't a burden, or someone's condition that must be offered up. Simply, he was her daily joy. There was a group of young activists singing American socialist songs from the 1930s late at night on the streets outside a political art club. They were gregarious in their welcome and spoke of their plans for a protest and their work fighting inequality, the growing darkness across the continent, and seeing the value of different people in their complicated culture. Their motto, *Meglio porco che fascista!* (better a pig than fascist), is a line borrowed from the Hayao Miyazaki film *Porco Rosso*. Porco was a character whose personality could at best be described as Gordian, but still there was a decency that couldn't be snuffed out. Sicily isn't Shang-ri-la. It is closer to Prospero's island that has had illusions set upon it by strong forces. It can give you whiplash with its quick pivot from beauty to ugly and back again.

It was on the beach in Mondello that my friend received a text from an old Italian work colleague in England asking where we were. This simple question led us to being introduced to this colleague's daughter and her friends, who were celebrating a recent graduation from university. The conversation immediately became about food, family and adventures. They explained the appeal of panelle (or, as they called it in Sicilian, *paneddi*), which is a kind of chickpea fritter served with bread. It is a food that belongs to everyone, from the poorest to the wealthiest. Everyone can agree on this dish. The daughter also said it is best eaten late at night after a few drinks. They gave us a suggestion for a restaurant for dinner and a path to wonderful interactions.

Dinner found us eating communally with two cousins. They were also celebrating: one had just finished getting his degree. They were obviously very close. We chatted about family, work, travel, gelato, food and beaches. I thought of my cousin Angela and our relationship: reminding each other what we are capable of and to be fearless with our love. If we are in the same city, it is an excuse to get together to eat. I thought of the trip I took with my brother Tom and Angela to the beaches of Normandy, and how we went on the longest walk whilst eating the best apricots and sipping cider straight from the bottle. Of sitting in an outdoor cafe eating a salad with the ripest tomatoes and rose. Of our night in Paris, eating falafel in the heat at the Marais and telling embarrassing stories about ourselves. Of sharing our good news, our anxieties, the bliss over the children we raise, the excitement over art, and our shared Jesuit/Buddhist beliefs when facing the challenges of self-doubt and the unspoken fears that live at the edge of our vision.

My relationship with Angela (along with each other's siblings) came as adults, as my father had kept us from much of his family.

I often wondered if he didn't want to introduce us because he feared that we might love them more or find that his misery wasn't something that should take up the whole room. When we did begin to meet my father's family there was an immediate familiarity and kinship. The truth was that my father had run away from the people who had adored and cared for him. I don't see his suffering as an insignificant thing. He had a mother who repeatedly abandoned him, and his sister (who was his one constant) was killed in a car accident in her late teens. Her death fractured the family for decades. But he always had family who adored him. His loving grandmother, who helped to raise him, died not knowing where he was. His anguish was so great, and my mother spent years encouraging him to make that shame less of a monster. He didn't want to show it the light or love.

Maybe he feared the idea that he had wasted years being captured by a dolor that wasn't so powerful. His family—my family—are such a gift. When we were together for lunch the day after my cousin Kathleen's wedding, we were talking in our usual way with hands and jokes flying about, and the server came up and said, "My goodness, I can tell all of you are related." And that night at that communal table in Palermo I saw two cousins who had the same shorthand with each other. They provided a parting gift: directions to a small bar where we would be taken care of by a very good barman.

With the kisses and cheer from brief dining companions to guide us on our way, we found the smallest of bars that spilled out onto the narrow streets and random conversations were formed. A chat with a man who told us how he was German and Tunisian and how his parents met. He veered between German, English and Italian like an acrobat. Then we came to know the bartender who insisted we have a drink together (compliments to his beautiful negronis led the way to such generosity). His best friend popped up and made a passionate declaration that his friend was the best bartender in Palermo. Maybe the occasional free drink makes for a solid friendship? He was right, though; his friend the bartender was fantastic at making drinks and bringing people together. In

Palermo, a city that some view with suspicion or write off as too disorganized, I possessed the most carefree smile. Amidst music, food, art, decay, history, noise, lecherous comments and feral cats, I felt a sea-change. The suffering was long ago.

§

The Akan believe that to achieve "personhood" one must take agency and be responsible for one's choices. There are some who are viewed as broken or not fully a person. But it isn't as if the individual is considered a complete lost cause or not worthy of support. The community must determine how responsible someone is for their state. There could be so many factors that can make it a challenge for a person. They could have been born at a disadvantage; they could have emotional problems, or have experienced terrible luck. There is recognition that not everyone is born with equal opportunity and some circumstances are beyond their control or responsibility. Such people are still considered a valued part of the community and worthy of care and respect. The great defining part of personhood is to have empathy beyond one's bloodline and to apply that same care to the well-being of the community. But there are those who wither away from the trees that could shelter them.

Every single morning in Sicily, I would wake up and feel a strange and familiar comfort. My sister described the same feeling when she stayed with our great uncle and watched him cook. She said it was like watching our father in the kitchen. The same mannerisms, the same approach to cooking. She said she kept waiting for the evening to descend into pandemonium and upset. The only discord would arrive in the form of our uncle putting more whipped cream on his pie than he should and our aunt objecting to it. If there is anyone who has achieved personhood, it is our uncle. He has witnessed so much turmoil in our family, yet he continues to offer everyone affection, humour and ice cream.

For me, it was fennel. It grows wild all over the island. Every single time I passed some being sold in the market I would stroke the downy fronds. I kept choosing it on the menu. In *pasta con le sarde* the larger fronds are used to flavour the pasta water, and then the bulb is sliced up and sautéed with the sardines and currants. It was the taste of the shoreline, and my childhood. Wild fennel grew outside my father's restaurant and he would use it in all kinds of dishes. It was the garnish to everything. He was good at putting wild weeds to use. It was from my cousin Angela that I discovered that my father had learned these skills from his family. Her father and my grandfather would go out together and forage edible greens to cook up in a stew pot. They had learned this from their mother, and so on. This is the truest part of Sicilian food. Like stone soup, meals can be cobbled together from the humblest ingredients. While others could afford to sprinkle Parmesan on their pasta, here they sprinkled toasted breadcrumbs (*pan grattato*). It adds a little more texture and another layer to what might be a simple meal. Every meal I ate became a culinary necromancy, as each bite showed me a little more of my father. A man who was terrified of personhood.

My ancestral town isn't Enna, where Persephone would reappear from the underworld, but it had its own sorcery. There was another strange visit from animals. We began to drive up into the hills in the middle of the island and a white dog appeared and kept trying to stop the car as its growling grew and grew. We eventually passed it and then we found another white dog who began to bark and chase the vehicle. We came to the bridge and discovered it was impassable. (It helps if the bridge is a complete bridge.)

This meant a new path. A tiny back road that had switchbacks that lead us higher and higher until we spotted the remains of a Norman castle. Like a salmon swimming against the current and leaping through the ladders, I had arrived home. To everyone here, this was my home. I had repeated conversations all over Sicily where I would be asked, "Where is your family from?" I would explain where they live now and they would say, "No, here. You are one of us, aren't you?" I would mention the town and they would all say, "Welcome home." As if I had been away for a little bit. And then I was home. Greeted by strangers in the familiar versus the formal.

Then there was lunch in a restaurant. Laughter with an older couple at the next table because we kept picking the same dishes (and asking each other how we liked it). Witnessing an extended family celebrating the baptism of the new baby. The newest member of the family and other young children were passed around and given attention while enjoying each course. The noise and energy of the children wasn't seen as a burden at the table. It was the thriving energy of family. A *nonna* singing to a little one, an uncle teaching a game to a niece and nephew, a father holding his baby daughter with great care so his wife could eat with two hands and talk to her sister, everyone discussing the service, how the priest did, the football, and what should they have for dinner.

It was time to leave and have a strange and winding journey through roads that barely existed. I was to head towards the southern shore. The whole drive down from the hills, it felt like I was slowly released from another spell both intimate and foreign. I landed in San Leone, near Agrigento. I visited the Kolymbetra—a hidden garden next to the Valley of the Temples, first formed by the arrival of the Arabs, who brought their irrigation and farming techniques along with their plants from native lands. They turned the remains of a lake into a lush garden full of fruits, vegetables, nuts and sugar cane. It passed through various hands and was the sort of place that romantic poets liked to wander through while on a tour with a mistress, evading bills and scandal. It was one of the few places that Lord Byron didn't sully. I like to think it wouldn't have been worthy of him, as he found eating to be an abomination and this was a place to have every sense nourished.

By the end of the twentieth century the garden was neglected but it was revived once again. I was lost to the luscious scents brought out by the heat in this hidden paradise. A community of people felt this place mattered and saw its potential value, and it bloomed in multiple ways. The groves of olives, almonds, lemons, limes and oranges of all kinds. Everything was offered. There was even a persimmon tree. I saw a bird with a large beak hopping about the edge, and I could picture it enjoying the soft candy sweet fruit that appears when Demeter says goodbye to her daughter once again. Not everything can be, or wants to be, restored from neglect. But I had always found the sun, a reason to awaken, a path to go towards, and had occasionally let others tend to me when I most needed it.

Then came the restaurant in San Leone. It was just like my father's. A glassed-in area where you could stay warm and still hear the waves. Where there were regulars who played cards and knew each other's lives. The easy manner of the servers who didn't just bring you food but extra conversation. Any discussion about the menu was almost political in terms of persuasion.

"Yes, this is nice, but really you want that."

Teasing encouragement to try one more thing. The owner would come out and talk to people. The chef would show off photos on his phone of his latest experiments in the kitchen in between making pizza or seafood. Even though I was full, I knew I had to try his cannolo. Then the lure to have drinks with the servers. Just one. Very small. It is a tiny bit of limoncello at most. Followed by giggles and chatter. Each night it was the same. Each night that peculiar feeling of recalling seafood eaten with people I once knew very well, of holding a baby who belonged to one of the regulars, of trying my father's special, and him coming out to talk to people who knew his food well. That warm place that once meant a lot.

My sister says she has mixed emotions when it comes to calamari. It was something our dad introduced to her as a child, and it was this wonderful memory. It is still something she loves to eat, but then she also remembers who he was and how he treated all of us. Over time I have come up with an answer to these memories: "Remember, I hate raw onions in just about any dish. I remove the onions and keep the dish. I don't toss it out and starve. Dad preferred starving. It is a terrible aching that makes you feel so lonely. I refuse to go hungry."

❦

The Mogya and Ntoro that the Akan receive from their parents are thought to travel with people throughout their lives. I carry two parts that always want to duel. I accept that there won't be peace. One side must be fed to thrive, and the other must be fed to quiet its cries of pain. A friend asked me, "How do you live with anger without diminishing it?" I thought of the city of Catania. In the seventeenth century, Etna erupted and wrecked the surrounding areas, and then there was an earthquake in 1693 that destroyed the city. They began to build with the lava stone from Etna. It gave it a distinctive identity and look, and they embraced the wedding cake-like detail of the Baroque style of architecture. When the artist I met in Catania had her studio set on fire a few weeks later, and all seemed impossible, people came to help her place recover and come alive again. Let all those feelings fuel you. You can make something a million times more beautiful and interesting, and let others see your anger plainly. You can take the simple things in the pantry and make a meal, but if you invite others in you can have a feast together. My father taught me how to draw others in at the table, but I had to learn that I should let others into the kitchen to see the mess and help me clean it up when I am overwhelmed. They always return for more.

Someone I loved once gave me a box full of darkness.
It took me years to understand that this too, was a gift.
– Mary Oliver

ℰ

HOPEFUL FROZEN DREAMS

Blackberry rhubarb sorbet represents the eternal hope that much of the British public has each May: that THIS year will be that good summer. That magical perfect summer where people get to look mildly beautiful (one of the unspoken truths about Britain is that the white natives only get a couple of good summers of being mildly beautiful, maybe); there will be a couple of good sexual awakenings that might be fodder for a memoir or collection of poetry in late middle age; the sandwiches won't be disappointing; and people might actually tan without having to first journey through purgatory with a lobster burn. Most of those dreams will be out of reach, but there is this sorbet, which will allow a person to celebrate a simple pure pleasure for a little bit while watching the sun being chased away by a periwinkle sky.

Let's imagine you have easy access to rhubarb, and you look forward to this moment in spring. (Or the actual reality is that the damn plant got out of hand again because it has been raining most of April and nothing will keep it under control and you are tired of making crumble and you know that no one really likes rhubarb jam all that much.) Or you have a neighbour who leaves it on your doorstep. The neighbour who does the same thing in high summer with courgettes. Courgette drive-bys were a common feature of my childhood. Sometimes I wondered if there were only eight courgettes in the whole town and people were trying to rid themselves of the bag of courgettes like it was a changeling child born during a blood moon. Let's get to work on it.

Chop up three cups of rhubarb (two or three stalks at most). Then you will toss that into a saucepan with three cups of blackberries. It is too early in May/June for blackberries, so you can buy a bag of frozen ones. (Or you are an incredibly well-organized person that has some in your freezer from blackberry picking last year. Most of us are not those people. It is okay. Freezers hold many secrets.) Then you will add one and a half cups of caster sugar. You will cook the fruit over medium heat, stirring here and there while you pause to look at the man working in the field who awoke something strange in you when you passed each other on the path. He said hello in a way that upset you, though you returned his greeting. Reduce the heat and let things cook until the rhubarb is quite soft.

Once everything is cooked, you will add a tablespoon of honey. (This will help with keeping things scoop-able after you churn everything and it is in the freezer. Trust me, it works.) Then you will want to purée everything. (Blender, food processor, stick blender—any of those work.) After that you will strain the blackberry rhubarb mix. This will get rid of the seeds. It can be fun to pick seeds out of your teeth, but not with this sorbet. Chill the fruit mix in the fridge for a couple of hours. Now we must divide people up. Some people have ice cream makers. If you do, churn the purée, put it in a container in the freezer and—ta-da, sorbet. If you lack a machine, you can take the purée, put it in a freezer-safe container and put it in the freezer. After half an hour take it out, churn/mix with a fork, return it to the freezer and then do that a few more times. (You can work on your poetry while you wait for things to firm up.) Then you will have sorbet.

Now for the final uncomfortable truth: the sandwiches always will be disappointing.

ROUND BREAD FOR SQUARE HANDS

My mother has small hands that are square with short fingers. Her entire life and work have been because of those unassuming hands. They have come to defy her in recent years, as she has developed Dupuytren's contracture. (She loves to brag about having 'Viking disease' because she says it sounds so metal.) In her obstinate way she continues to make them work for her. She finds and creates a new pattern or rhythm and takes off because she isn't done.

Those hands first experienced their fate in piano lessons. She had begun playing things by ear and it was decided she needed to learn properly. "I hated to practise." My mother is a woman who doesn't lie or attempt to dress up a challenge or hardship as a noble opportunity to find grace in some sort of martyrdom. She wasn't nostalgic about the early years of learning. Her tenacity was what kept her practising. An emotional trait that resides within women in the family: utter frustration and anger, but a rabid desire to understand and conquer a puzzle. Most people don't go beyond a couple of years of lessons before giving up. My mom trained to be a pianist—quite the occupation with those little hands. Stretching to those far-off keys with a flat-fingered playing approach (a bit like Horowitz, to put her in refined company). In adolescence she would practise around eight hours a day, all while going to school. She was beginning to get paying gigs, and she was doing competitions. But then there was one competition where the same young man won two years running, playing "Moonlight Sonata". She commented, "A piece most of us learn when we were ten. He didn't add any new or original interpretation to it. He merely played it correctly. I quickly figured out they weren't going to give it to a girl. I decided not to compete anymore."

I never knew this story until one visit where we spent much of our time discussing classical music and bread baking (two subjects on which she knows a great deal). She was so keen to show me how to make this bread that she felt made for excellent toast, but the real excitement had to do with the fact that it didn't require kneading. While telling me this story of music, she dissolved one tablespoon of yeast into about four ounces of warm water and set it to prove in a large bowl, pointing out that unlike most no-knead breads it wasn't going to create a door stop that aggravated jaw conditions when chewing. It was complete lightness. She said, "I always think of the wretched bread served in vegetarian restaurants in the seventies. No one knew how to adjust for liquid and fats, and everything was so dry and heavy. Those were the dark ages that no one talks about." There are always stories when she teaches me to cook anything. Into the same bowl with the proven yeast, she poured about eight ounces of milk ("Never skim milk; we don't hate people. Plus you need that bit of fat to make it work"), two ounces of sugar, two teaspoons of salt, and then mixed in three large eggs and four ounces of softened butter: "If you dare put in margarine we may need to disown you." She mixed that until smooth and added, "I won an award for this."

My mother's perseverance takes her many places; she doesn't give up on competition easily. Just watch her mark the booklet for the county fair home arts section as she figures out all the different categories she can enter. Or glance at her collection of ribbons acquired over the decades in areas devoted to baking, sewing, knitting, and food preservation (even at the state fair level). She also does not waste her time trying to win over people who refuse to see her talents or dismiss them as ephemeral women's work. She learned this one at the hands of her parents, who treated her (to borrow her phrase) as "the auxiliary back-up child" in deference to her brother, who was the golden boy who possessed great talents such as having bad luck with cars (either wrecking them or having them stolen), standing in front of the house smoking, and being upwardly successful for a mediocre man. Her piano-playing was considered a nice accomplishment for a woman to have (something to show off to company, or entertain at parties). It wasn't viewed as a potential career to support. Years of effort, only to be told, "But it doesn't really matter." She didn't listen. She went on to learn voice, teaching herself to transpose, along with a million other skills (and instruments). She made music a career that has supported her for over forty years in the most diverse ways. Her hands carried all this work and talent, and it wasn't going to wither.

In the kitchen she added four to five ounces of bread flour to the batter. "You have to kind of eyeball it. It depends on how the batter is feeling that day. We all have our moods." She mixed before handing it over to me and saying, "Be kind to your old mother and put your hands to work." I am happy to do this task. It reminds me of when she would have me stir the jam, which would take forever as it boiled, so she could tend to a million other tasks. But today she returns to her knitting and looks at the news online, irritated by one more awful person interfering with the lives of other women, commenting, "Damned if you, damned if you don't." Once the batter dough was smooth and met her expectations, we covered it and let it sit to rise for an hour.

In her youth, everyone was discovering the kitchen. Nearly everyone in her generation had a copy of *The Tassajara Bread Book* (her ancient edition remains in a tattered state next to *The Beard Bread Book*). It wasn't enough just to learn to make a loaf of bread. She wanted to make very good bread. She was drawn to childhood memories of reading *Little House* books by Laura Ingalls Wilder and all the food mentioned throughout the stories, and fantasies of having her own farmstead as she kneaded that bread. Then she had to try and bake breads from various cultures. She didn't have the money to travel. There wouldn't be a farmstead. There was work. Later on there were children. But she kept mastering things. Understanding the chemistry and the subtleties in each creation. Those hands kneaded hundreds of loaves. There was so much strength. I would watch her as a child as she would take the sticky dough and fold it, push it, and turn it with authority. It was hypnotic to my eyes. I remember being about seven and asking to knead. She showed me how. My hands, while large (and having the same squareness as hers), were not as capable. "You have to put all of your strength into it. You have to keep working on it." I got tired after a few minutes and gave up. She said, "You don't get to do that when kneading bread. You have to keep going. Even when it is hard. Then it will turn out well." Taking over again to knead, she would make it look simple.

"You don't get to punch down this dough like it's that one person you hate, but it is fun to stir." She stirred the risen dough down for me while telling me about how she loves Mendelssohn even though he isn't all that fashionable. Her work in music led her to playing for choirs and eventually leading choirs. She encouraged me to listen to his oratorio "Elijah". She gave an impassioned description of the depth of feeling that was in the piece and why it was unusual: it has elements of Baroque but is by a Romantic composer. Her taste has always favoured the Romantics over Baroque. (Unless of course it is Bach. Bach can do no wrong in her eyes. He wrote powerful work and was always trying to get a better paying gig that gave him more control over what he did.) Baroque is technically pretty and very correct. Romantic music has a kind of wildness that grabs my mother's soul. The composers were not afraid to display vulnerability across the keyboard.

She had me get out a tubed tin and grease it for her. She then spooned the batter into the tin. She covered it once again and let it sit for another hour. It gave her time to tell me more stories of the family, to tell me the history of a favourite rabbit breed, to tell me about her love of a Masai farmer's Twitter account, why I ought to watch this one film, to tell me about an art exhibition involving indigenous women and why I needed to see it, to tell me about a dark and hilarious Russian folktale she read, and then finish with how to grow dahlias when the slugs are on the rampage. In one hour she can take you places while she sits still in her chair, with a single pause to ask for more coffee.

Now it was time to bake! The oven was ready at 390°F/200°C. The bread went in for about 25–30 minutes. (Ovens can be fiddly and choose to run hot like a woman in the presence of her lover, racing to be undone even before the taxi driver has been paid. In both cases someone is bound to yelp, "Already? Quick! Out!" So keep a close eye on things. The bread shouldn't be too toasty.) When it was removed from the oven, my mother admired it for a moment like it was a baby. "Isn't it lovely?" It needed a little assistance in being loosened from the tin. It was a ring of perfect bread. She sliced through it and revealed something soft and buttery. Everyone felt greedy for it right away. We didn't want to wait for it to properly cool. "Does it need butter?" "Well, it doesn't, but it is still a good idea to add some because butter is so good." My mother's Scandinavian roots show deep in that sentence. We don't require *tandsmør* (tooth butter—when butter is applied so thickly onto a slice of bread that it leaves tooth marks when a bite is taken), but just enough to feel elevated by the taste and texture of this delightful bread. As there are grandchildren about, it goes quickly. All her bread disappears into the ether at such speed. Growing up with my siblings, we would go through it as if we were being timed. My mother would come home to find the bread gone and she would mutter, "You guys need to warn me when you are going to have another toast orgy."

My mother's curiosity is a kind of appetite that doesn't fade or dwindle. She has never been one to say, "I've had enough," or lie delicately on a chaise, declaring, "Oh, I only digest these things." She has always understood Patrick Dennis's *Auntie Mame*, who told her nephew, "Life is a banquet and most poor bastards are starving to death!" She has little patience with certain types of people who wish to tell her about the offerings on the table of life, especially when they act like they built the table and invented the offerings. Explaining things as if she just appeared and was trying rice cereal for the first time. The ones who wish to tell her about music: how they have been playing a bit and never felt they needed to learn to read music. The ones who tell her that the bread she makes is quaint, but real baking involves rustic artisan bread that they just discovered and they could tell her how to make one day. She doesn't bother to smile. Her smile is worth too much to waste on opinions paraded as important information. She might offer the most dispassionate of her phrases, "That's nice," before returning to the table and being taken with something exciting, or new, or strange.

After making us bread she is onto the next thing and begins talking about how she wants to make a cheese cracker that has cumin and ancho chilies because she was inspired by something she had eaten at a potluck after the Spanish language mass she plays for, or how she has been writing honky-tonk music and lyrics about murder kept coming to her when she was in the queue at the grocery store. She pulls out the little notebook that lives in her handbag and holds it in her wonderfully worn hands that have become more like her mother's over time (even decorated with the same rings). "Does anyone have a pen? I wonder what else I could add to the crackers. Pork? Ooh, what about lime?" Now we wait. Mom has ideas again!

UNTO YOU THERE ARE NIBBLES

Some may choose to purify themselves in the waters of Lake Minnetonka but the wisest of Minnesotans knows the truest path to the promised land is found via a cheese ball. Have you heard the good word? Gather round, children, for I shall bring you to L'Etoile du Nord with its fine party spreads. The cheese ball is based on apocryphal tales of Thomas Jefferson receiving a giant one, but what we of Midwestern ancestry know for sure is that a woman out of Minnesota appeared with a recipe and it was good.

We must pause and give thanks and praise to the women of the Midwest. From home economists who were coming up with ways to improve the lives of women and ease their labour, to the housewives who were filled with the spirit of creativity and improvisation, they brought us many gifts which we overlook and don't entirely deserve (but they give them to us anyway because they don't want us to go hungry).

At times people will show discomfort around the cheese ball. Lo, Arne Carl will deny that cheese ball three times in San Francisco, but come Christmas he will scarf down his Aunt Dorothy's cheese ball like a starving man. We don't judge. Not everyone can be strong and of good courage.

Yes, there may be hesitation when that round coated object surrounded with crackers (like patient acolytes) is presented to the uninitiated or the cynical sophisticates with their ironic appreciation of aspics. You will be asked, "What exactly is this?" or someone will say, "Oh ... how kitsch." Instead of hate, celebrate. Offer them hospitality. Hand one of them the knives and say, "Let's take a page from Kierkegaard and not hurry past pleasure."

As you refresh their drinks their conversion will be swift. It isn't an orthodox experience where the old life must be forsaken. There won't be multiple volumes of confession and regret. One shall be like Norsemen who adopted various elements of a culture. Cheese is ecumenical. Soon you will have people wanting to be like the apostles, wandering to the far ends of the empire to bring this goodness to one and all. You take them to the temple that is your kitchen and say, "Get a bowl. And a spatula."

Offer thanks to Aristaeus and then combine six ounces of grated Double Gloucester with chives and onion, and seven ounces of softened cream cheese. (If you are unable to get hold of Double Gloucester with chives and onion, get yourself some without the frills, and add one tablespoon of onion granules and one tablespoon of dried chives.) Then add one teaspoon of smoked paprika, one teaspoon of celery seed, half a teaspoon of chervil, one clove of garlic, minced, and one tablespoon of Worcestershire sauce. Everything will come together as if part of some great union of joy. Form it into a ball, wrap it up in cling film and pop it in the fridge for a couple of hours to firm up.

Do take care with new disciples. They are filled with zeal for this new life and will want to fall deep into the world of cheese balls and to bring others into the fold. Encourage their creativity. After all, some things in their natural state have the most *vivid* colors. But gently remind them that not everyone loves cheese that much, and some are not ready to come of their own free will.

Now to finish up the cheese ball. Remove it from the fridge and then either roll it around in about eight ounces of finely chopped pecans, or if people are unable to eat nuts you can roll it around half a cup of freshly chopped parsley. Your alchemy will be rewarded with love and adoration. Let this combination of cheese bind everyone together in perfect unity.

PICNIC GUIDE FOR
YOUR SEXUAL AWAKENING

You awake to find the sun high in the sky, displaying the full radiance of its glow like a dominant peacock. Common sense says that the sun is not to be trusted, for it has a history of causing ruin. The warmth creeps in quietly and coaxes you with unspoken ideas and promises that are far away from the chapel-like safety of the indoors. That virginal sanctum, with its offerings of air-conditioning and carefully chilled food. It may be safe and appropriate, like a man with a good reputation and income, but you are led by a doomed avidity to eat out of doors, surrounded by the splendour of nature's living temple. Yes, it's a good day to experience a sexual awakening whilst on a picnic. But before you race outside with your wicker basket full of sandwiches, and a bewildering want that must be satiated, you need to consider a few things and pack accordingly.

Your picnic must be in a field. Sexual awakenings can't be found on beaches. (Unless you are Italian.) You may have sex on the sand, but you should have already established what you are about. Parking lots are where middle-aged salesmen named Gary eat day-old egg salad sandwiches before flashing their lights to go dogging. A field provides the right opportunity to cast off the obligations of society and convention. Just beware of ticks.

At least one member of the party needs to be repressed in some fashion if this is going to work. They ought to feel uneasy or constrained by life but recognize (and maybe even distrust) the feral angry beauty in their surroundings. (Ideally a Russian lit major, or someone who studied Divinity but has recently experienced an existential crisis and now works with their hands.) Even if you have participated in a few orgies at art school, you can still find a repressed side of yourself (like the shame you experience because you fancy an elected official that you rationally despise).

Now let's have a look through the basket. The biggest rule is don't bring macaroni salad. Or scotch eggs, because you might as well pack up your genitals in Tupperware and go home. You want foods that deepen in flavour as they await your touch, and which must be carefully pulled apart with your fingers, teeth and lips (think of cheeses, soft fruits, and carefully decorated tarts).

To really set the tone, bring a steamed artichoke. It appears unyielding and carefully closed in—possibly like your chosen guest. And again, like your chosen guest, that artichoke needs something to bring it alive. Mayonnaise doesn't inspire any sensuality. Aioli does. This is an important distinction when choosing a condiment to have with your steamed artichoke.

You begin by pulling off each leaf. The first ones will be quite firm and lack much flavour. The aioli will glide along the meat and bring it to life. As you and your guest eat, the artichoke will give more flesh. Carefully turn the conversation from the weather to Artsybashev's shameless approach to man's desires, or the dichotomy of being and nothingness.

You will want to pause and take in the scene. Listen to the susurration of the surrounding life and gaze upon the delicate unfurled wildflowers. Like the artichoke, all is nearly undone, but first you must go through the violaceous petals and pileous choke to reach that most yielding heart. By this point, if you have choreographed everything correctly and it hasn't started to rain (though you can use this to your advantage by running with the other person to an ancient ruin, or a cave), one should be overcome with a primal cupidity. For a moment everything that you once knew or felt will be as scattered and used up as the bitten artichoke petals.

Afterwards, as you lie on the picnic blanket, slowly becoming aware of the rock pressing into your back, you will notice the flies on the oozing cheese that has sat too long, and the berries that are bruised and dull, leaving a sticky sheen to things. There are no wet wipes. A heartless metaphor for the malaise that follows such a release.

FARAWAY SCENT OF PAIN

The Cook felt she should have the final say when all could rest in her kingdom. She poked the remains of coal that resembled small, rough pieces of salted liquorice, wanting to urge a little more labour from them. It wasn't going to be enough to warm the often angry range. A bit more coal was going to be required to charm enough heat for one final cup. Thankfully her mistress never questioned the amount of coal used by the kitchen staff. She would do a kindness to Norah by clearing the ashes herself. (The Cook also didn't want Norah to ask why there were more ashes on a night when there had only been a light supper for her ladyship.)

The dusty Assam tea for the staff had no more flavour or colour to give after several brews, and the Cook tossed it into the kitchen waste. Instead, she chose to treat herself to a single spoonful of the Darjeeling that her mistress took each day at four. It was just the one or two cups of the subtle floral drink. Not enough to cause any curiosity when inventory was done, but then it was the Cook who gave those final numbers to the butler, Mr Blackthorn, a man who appreciated a spoonful of that same tea every Tuesday and Thursday at five-thirty. The Cook began preparations by bringing out her own small tea service. (A gift from her sister who had had the fortune to marry an artist in a pottery.) As the kettle began to heat up, she brought out a wooden caddy that was covered in faded flowers that had been painted years ago by a child. She was smelling the contents of the caddy when Norah came to the doorway. The Cook noticed the scullery maid was without her cap but decided not to say anything at this hour.

Norah said, "Beg your pardon, Mrs Spindle. Her ladyship will be here directly. She desires to make Master Tarquin his favourite." Mrs Spindle shut the caddy and put it on the buffet. They would need more coal. And not just for the tea.

The small dancing light of her ladyship's candle made its way down the kitchen hall and brought with it a pallid woman in a tired shawl of Indian pink silk. Lady Hartland always carried with her a candle when travelling the house at night. She had never come to truly trust the gas lighting installed twenty-five years previous. She claimed her candle was much more reliable than "that leaking vapour", which she was convinced was the cause of all cases of dropsy.

Lady Hartland said, "Good evening, Mrs Spindle. I hate to bother you, as I am sure you must be quite busy. But you do understand ... "

The Cook replied, "Of course, your Ladyship. Anything for Master Tarquin. Norah, fetch the rice, and sugar. And bring us a pan of water. Ma'am, please sit while we ready everything."

Norah, who was still quite new to the house, was confused by this visitor and this talk of busyness. The only thing on the range was a kettle, the table was scrubbed and clear of the daily paraphernalia (minus the Cook's tea service), and the other members of the kitchen staff had gone to bed. Norah had been on her way as well when she had encountered Lady Hartland on the back stairs. Her Ladyship was a supernatural being to a scullery maid who spent her days confined to a few rooms, always trying to catch up with Mrs Spindle's directions. This one made little sense, but she obeyed like someone who hoped to one day become a parlour maid.

Lady Hartland, noticing the modest tea things laid out, asked, "Goodness, Mrs Spindle, have I interrupted your tea-time?"

Mrs Spindle quickly answered, "Not at all, ma'am. We thought you might like some. Since the pudding does take a bit of time and we wouldn't want you to lose your energy."

"You sound like my governess. Where is the tea? What are we having? Is it Oolong? Or that schoolroom Assam. Let me smell the tea."

The Cook opened the caddy and handed it to her mistress. Lady Hartland smiled and said, "I still am so proud of my sweet Tarquin for painting this. This Darjeeling is perfect. I think of the journeys up to the hill station each year with my ayah, and my two brothers. I suppose mother was there. Somewhere." She shared memories and stories that the Cook had heard before but were new to Norah, who listened carefully as she laid out ingredients. There had been a home surrounded by a garden that was greener and more prodigious than anything ever seen in England, playing with the servants, rare visits by Father, and being soothed by her ayah with lullabies and puddings. Lady Hartland handed the caddy to Norah and said, "We saw my mother every single evening at 5pm. Just after she had her tea and just before she was to have a little rest before dressing for dinner. If we were fortunate, she might give us some bread and butter. I preferred what my ayah would make. Do we have enough coal to make pudding, and tea? What is your name? Oona? Norah? Fetch us some."

Mrs Spindle found no reason to object to her Ladyship's generosity with the coal at this hour. Norah helped to build up the fire while Lady Hartland continued to talk and speak of Master Tarquin's illness and how he wouldn't eat unless it was the rice pudding his mother would make for him. Mrs Spindle led Lady Hartland to the range and supervised as her Ladyship poured everything into the pot and stirred it with a spoon and shared more news with the servants. "I don't know if Nanny has told you if he is on the mend? He has been such a brave soul."

Norah, while sweeping up the coal dust and listening to the chatter, forgot the temporary rules of formality with their guest and asked, "Nanny?"

The Cook gave her that firm maternal look demanding immediate silence. Norah could be forgetful but she knew when to retreat. Lady Hartland continued, "My ayah came with us on the ship when it was time to leave India. I was fortunate to have an extra year at home as Mother wanted to wait until my youngest brother could go. We spent so long at sea I thought I was going to become a pirate. When we arrived in England, we were sent to our Aunt Agnes. Ayah didn't come with us. We were told she had other children to care for now. We thought this meant Mother was to be with us. She told us she was to return to India. My brothers cried for her not to leave. My mother told us, 'A woman can have another woman tend to her children, but she can't have another woman tend to her husband.' We never had the chance to say goodbye to my ayah." She stopped stirring and covered the pan with a lid and became silent.

The Cook directed Norah to bring milk for tea and pudding. The scullery maid disappeared into the cold room along with her broom. Lady Hartland came back to the present and asked, "Could you move the rice to a cooler place? I am feeling a bit faint." The Cook moved the pan while her ladyship sat at the large kitchen table. Lady Hartland waited as if she was a guest in Mrs. Spindle's home. The Cook filled the teapot with hot water to warm it before pouring it out and brewing the tea. She even made sure there was some for Norah, who stood to one side, afraid to sit. Lady Hartland admired Norah's ability to build up a fire. "It was so cold when I came home to England. I hated the pungent scent of coal smoke, but I would stay in the kitchen by the range to keep warm, or follow the maid about as she built fires. Later she taught me to build a fire. My friends at school were impressed that I could do such a thing. My Aunt Agnes did not think it was appropriate for me to show off, but she thought it was a sensible skill so that I could tell if a servant wasn't good at their tasks. I don't believe she told my parents what I had been learning. When I was twelve, my parents came home on leave. I had not seen them in years, and I wanted them to see how much I had grown. My father was horrified that I knew how to lay a fire. He told my aunt and mother that I would end up a spinster, and I needed to learn to be a lady. Any boring Edith can do needlework; I can still lay a fire, and I did so earlier for Master Tarquin as he was so very cold."

Norah looked concerned, wondering if she had another grate to clean. Mrs Spindle glanced at the scullery maid and shook her head. She poured tea and asked Lady Hartland, "Milk? I know you do not take sugar."

"Oh, dear Mrs Spindle, let's have sugar. Norah too." The Cook followed directions and there was tea fit for a nursery. Her ladyship regained her strength and stood up once again. She found that the rice and sugar had cooked down, then added milk. The reviving tea made it possible for her to move the pan and begin to stir once again. "Father was wrong. I didn't end up a spinster aunt carrying her tatting from room to room. It was decided that I should have a governess. Miss Lund. She was Danish but she could speak French and German. Supposedly she had taught some minor count's daughters. She taught me how to make this. She felt that even a lady should be able to do something in the kitchen. She said it would cure most minor maladies and make ill-tempered children behave. The year before I came out, she quite surprised us when she announced that she was to be married. It was a wonderful scandal. Her intended was the younger brother of her former employer the Count! He was also quite a bit younger than she."

Norah and Mrs Spindle were pouring more of her ladyship's tea and taking turns to refill the pot as they listened to Lady Hartland share every secret. Lady Hartland said, "We should have bread and butter. This is exhausting work to stir things." Norah was quick to get those, along with some jam. She was learning the art of anticipating possible needs. Mrs Spindle began to slice and butter bread while her ladyship continued.

"Miss Lund gave her notice, told me that painting china was for ladies without personality, and always to be polite to servants. She left on a boat to South Africa with this Count von Regenstein or Risengrød. We need more eggs and sugar very soon. This is beginning to look like porridge. My sweet boy is going to be so happy when we bring this to him. Miss Lund gave me one more gift. There was a touch of that scandal about me as I began to go to balls. I was the girl who had had that governess who had the arrogance to marry well. As if sensible Miss Lund had been a bad influence. Some asked me to waltz to find out if I was wicked. Engaged before the end of the season. My aunt sent Miss Lund a wedding gift. Often I have wondered if it was a thank you gift. Shall we do something with the eggs?"

Mrs Spindle, full of bread and jam, helped to separate the eggs. She knew she would have to do something with the whites in the morning. Lady Hartland whisked a few spoonfuls of the rice porridge into the egg yolks before pouring all of it into the pot along with a few more spoonfuls of sugar and a sprinkling of salt. It was soon thick like custard but so much better. Lady Hartland paused and said, "It needs something else. Otherwise Tarquin will not eat it. Spices! Do we have any vanilla bean? He likes speckles."

Mrs Spindle, putting dirtied dishes aside, paused. "Ma'am ... I am not entirely sure. We shall have to look through the cupboards."

Norah, still enjoying the scene, quickly brought many small tins to her ladyship before the Cook could provide the appropriate choices. Lady Hartland began to look at each tin and smell things. Curry, garden blend, turmeric, ginger, mace, cloves. Never quite it. She did love the saffron and remembered her ayah making a rice porridge with saffron and pistachios.

Then she found it. Nutmeg. The Cook watched. She knew the midnight feast was ending.

Lady Hartland opened the jar and smelled the nutmeg. She looked startled. She quickly set it down as if it had burned her fingers. Lady Hartland looked so confused and began to weep, trying to grab onto something and whispering, "My darling boy." The Cook put her arm around her ladyship and said, "I know, ma'am," and then told Norah, "Go and remove the pudding from the heat. You must go and wake her ladyship's maid Dearborn. Tell her that her mistress needs help being put to bed again." Norah was now privy to the world of upstairs and chose to be quick, out of curiosity—and discomfort with the growing tears of Lady Hartland. The Cook listened to her ladyship speak to no one in particular as she said, "My boy. He wanted his supper. How could I forget?" She led her down the hall and up the drafty stairs for servants. Dearborn met them and said she would provide a cordial to help her mistress sleep.

Norah asked about the candle. The Cook knew it could wait until morning, along with the egg whites. They made their way back down to the kitchen to tidy up from the impromptu party. The Cook said, "I should have warned you about Lady Hartland's spells. It has been a while. The nutmeg is what sets her off. I try and keep it out of the way. Master Tarquin died years ago, and she had a funny turn. Thinking he is still about. She is awake, but isn't. The doctor said to let her be so as not to upset the lady. Bless her. One never forgets a child. Her heart is a little more broken than some. Remind me to put the nutmeg in a faraway cupboard. Now miss, we must tidy. We shall have one more cup of tea, and then to bed."

Norah asked, "And the pudding?"

"The staff will be very lucky tomorrow to have some with their dinner. She won't remember what she has made, and we shall make the best of things. Have a taste; it is wonderful and cosy. Her ladyship isn't wrong—it is just the thing when you feel under the weather."

Norah tried a spoonful, and then another.

𝒞

AN INCOMPLETE GUIDE TO
DRINKERS OF SOME BLACK TEAS

Earl Grey

They don't always mean to make things complicated, but sometimes the world is a bit overwhelming and they require a bit more tenderness. Often very sweet, but you do need to be gentle or they might fall apart. Some might view them as prissy, or even snobbish at times (and some can be). Aesthetics are important to them and play heavily into finding comfort in their environment. Yes, it is tea that was invented to mimic a more expensive black tea (and they know this, thank you, they don't need that Darjeeling drinker pointing that out just to hurt their feelings) but they take delight in the perfume scent. Earl Grey drinkers are more inclined to ask for the tea in a specific cup. "Not that mug—that mug is better for coffee when you need the heat held for a long time. I just want a bit of tea, not too much. If you could, please, I would like to have my tea in that vintage cup with the hand-painted scene of a Welsh cottage. I bought that cup and saucer after I left that awful job that gave me stress hives. Also, no sugar, please, as it takes over the flavour of the tea, and just a bit of milk—whole only. Skimmed ruins the colour of everything and makes it look like dishwater and then I can't drink it." They will always say please and thank you for the effort you put into making things pleasing. They will always remember how you like your tea, and quietly assign you a cup of your own to let you know they think of you. They may not always make your birthday party, but they do thoughtful things like send you random gifts (often the perfect thing you never realised you needed). The blankets in their homes are always soft.

Lady Grey

They are prissy and are the first ones to declare they have the flu when they actually have a cold. Lady Grey was a recent invention because some people thought Earl Grey was too much. If it was the nineteenth century, they would be the sort to languish for years on a chaise and somehow outlive all their relations who were in very good health.

Darjeeling

I wouldn't come out and say that they are edgelords, but they are the first to pick a fight. They are well known for their passive aggressive comments about lapsang souchong: "It's like drinking burnt rope. I suppose they also enjoy wearing hair shirts." They do have well-informed opinions about a variety of subjects and think that not only should they have very good things, but everyone else should too (which is lovely, but not everyone likes the same thing as everyone else). They become downright annoyed when people don't listen and have the nerve to go and buy that inferior version of shoe or fridge after explaining why the other one is worth the investment. After all, their tea comes from a very specific place, and why have a knock-off when you can have something quality and beautiful that lasts? (If you ever want to shut them up, point out that most modern Darjeeling is more of an oolong.) Darjeeling drinkers can be charming and occasionally even sexy, but it doesn't always save them when they go off on a rant about how anyone who likes that particular thing is a complete fool and deserves to be mauled by a bear. The problem with Darjeeling drinkers is that they want someone to think they are special and wonderful, but they don't know how to say it without breaking half of the tea set and insulting someone's favourite book. They are reckless, well-meaning passion, in a cup that ends up with a few cracks.

Lapsang Souchong

They will always have a Gothic sensibility. They are into incense, have multiple collections of curios, will always be drawn to anything that is velvet, and likely have a cat named Polidori or Zinaida that sheds everywhere and yet is never seen. They don't like to tell you the complete story about anything, and you are left to wonder half of the time, "Wait … if she was married to Arturo, then who was that other man with the beard that she was living with in Budapest?" You won't encounter a great deal of argument from a lapsang souchong drinker. They just do things their own way, and if you don't like it, they will take it somewhere else. (They will point out to their friend the Darjeeling drinker that lapsang is likely the oldest black tea, and then change the subject to a collection of vintage comics they found at a car boot sale.) They are rarely on time. EVER. You have to lie to them about what time something starts so that they actually show up at the right time, and even then they still show up a little bit late. If they aren't wrapped up in the warmth of their home, they will be found out in the woods touching the bark of the trees, and trying to write a poem about the decay of the forest floor.

Russian Caravan (cousin to Lapsang)

These people are always romantics who have notions about living a nomadic life, sitting around a campfire at night, wearing the perfume of the smoke whilst seduced by the *duende* of the guitar player's music. They also like central heating and hot running water, so most things remain a fantasy, or a brief sojourn that allows them to have a story at dinner. They have a massive scarf collection—something for every occasion and mood. Velvet is nice, but they know that a poplin gauze will be more appropriate for a climb in the hills with their lover, who has the most bewitching eyes and says little. They will always defend Byron's behaviour, and they read Gogol for fun. Twice (the second time while staying in a warm dacha where someone's granny made the perfect blinis). They never brush their hair.

Assam

Most drinkers of this tea just want it strong and done, preferably by someone who calls them Love. Man? Woman? Doesn't matter. They just need something that will make them hear the universe breathe, smell colours, and allow them to face the day. Assam is sometimes referred to as the lion of teas. Really? It's the Jason Statham of teas. It has a weird history that it doesn't want to talk about, it will wreck you six different ways, and you will thank it for the privilege of experiencing its power. The tea has its own time, because, like its drinkers, it has stuff to get done. It doesn't have time to lark about with lattes. (They drink coffee in the evening to calm down, thank you.) Assam drinkers will stand about with the tea bag still in their cup, almost embracing the risk of burning the roof of their mouth. Sometimes they can go too far in showing off how little they need. Often they are the ones to end up in hospital with the flu or a lost spleen. "It's fine, don't know what the fuss was about. My mum got a bit worried when I passed out and hit my head on the toilet. Got back to it." They are the ones with stories about how they woke up at a festival having agreed to take a job with a professional gambler that ended up paying for a break in Barbados. "And that's how I got into a conversation with this chap who turned out to be Grandmaster Flash." You are never quite sure what is true with them and what isn't, but you are always amused and add another sugar (always two sugars and milk).

Irish Breakfast

Drinkers of this tea were historically seen as wasting time and being decadent. Frankly, they don't care what you think, because unless you plan on taking care of things, you can shut your mouth. Irish Breakfast drinkers may not seem organized to outsiders, but they get things done. The paperwork will be in the right place, the reservations for dinner will be made, and by the time you are brushing your teeth, they have a day out for twenty planned and a bus booked. They will always have a snack, and their bag is filled with things that everyone needs but always forgets. They may talk your ear off, but they also listen a lot and watch everyone around them. And they know everyone's business. You want to find out who is getting divorced, who is having a fight with whom, and every other bit of solid gossip? Talk to an Irish Breakfast tea drinker. They keep everything running but let others think they have the power.

Microwaved cup of Lipton Tea
This is a desperate cry for help. My God, my God, why have you forsaken me?

ℭ

YOU CAN'T GENTRIFY THIS

Faggot can refer to a bundle of sticks. Sometimes, in an abbreviated form, it is a junior student in a posh school who has the job of being some kind of lackey or sex slave to a senior student; each will trade on these initial experiences in his climb to become a member of government. It can even be a simple loving meal. There are so many utterings of faggots by the British, it is like being in a junior high locker room. Continuing that theme, let's have balls of faggots in our mouths.

This is not a dish that has been adopted by the affluent classes in their quest for authentic simplicity. Bitter greens? Of course. Casseroles? Put it in some Le Creuset and it's attractively rustic. Fish and chips? Add a bottle of Krug and it's amusing, like a 1930s hobo-themed party with the Rockefellers. But it can be difficult to find easy romance in the offcuts of meat mixed together with herbs and breadcrumbs. It isn't like a fling with someone your snobbish mother might refer to as well-spoken, who was gifted by the random luck of DNA with a rough form of good looks. This is kitchen sink realism where loyal people loan each other the same ten quid to get to the end of the week.

You aren't going to find faggots in a butcher shop run by earnest young men with beards who left their PhD in semiotics, where the cuts of meat come with stories of their Ellis Island-like journey to the shop. You are going to places where the men have hands covered in the scars of so many cuts and slices that the skin creates its own cuts and slices because that is what it knows. If you want to make your own faggots, you need those butchers, because they have what you need.

Chop up about four ounces of pork liver, four ounces of bacon, and a couple of lamb's kidneys (make sure they are rinsed and skinned) and place that in a bowl. Then melt a spoonful of meat drippings in a pan (if you can't handle meat drippings, you can't handle adulthood) and throw in a chopped onion, a tablespoon of sage, and a teaspoon of mace. You want the onions soft. While that's cooking you can contemplate life's disappointments. Take the onion/herb mixture and add that to your meats. Mix that together with a few tablespoons of breadcrumbs. Form into balls that should fit comfortably into your hands.

Now you need to spread out some beef caul. You will need quite a bit (maybe eight ounces), as you will likely fuck this up and create bigger holes. Carefully wrap some of the caul around each ball and then tuck the seam underneath. They should look a bit like brains that have been decorated with a lace scarf made by your nan. Melt some more fat in a pan and place the faggots in the pan. (Make sure where the caul wraps up is the side you cook first so everything stays together. This is another thing you will likely fuck up but it's okay.) You will brown them all over and then put them in a baking dish.

In that same frying pan, you will make a gravy. Gravy is what keeps people from killing themselves. There should be enough leftover fat from cooking the faggots that you can sauté another chopped-up onion. Add a tablespoon of vinegar and cook everything until the liquid evaporates. Sprinkle a tablespoon of plain flour over the onions and give it a quick stir so it coats the onions. You will then slowly add about a pint of beef stock. Not bone broth, but stock. Because everyone on this street will slap the shit out of you for saying something like bone broth.

Whisk until everything thickens. Add a splash of Worcestershire sauce and a little beer. You can eyeball how much is appropriate.

Season to taste. This is a gravy that could be a meal on its own. You will pour this all over your faggots, cover with a lid, or foil, and pop them in the oven at 350°F/180°C for about an hour. Remove the lid/foil and let things cook for another twenty minutes. Then remove from the oven.

Serve with mash and peas. Slather gravy over everything. For this pâté-like dish is fantastic and we must continue to keep people in the dark about it ... Shit. I fucked up by telling you assholes about it.

ℰ

PETTY CREAM TEA

Winifred Birkeland had never found the energy to embrace the enthusiasm required for a church fete, or a village quiz. She loved Angela Thirkell novels. Unfortunately, Thirkell hadn't prepared her for everything: namely Winifred's own macabre nature. "Jolly" wasn't her natural state. If she was ever unbridled it was on her terms, never at the altar of tombola and panto. Should anyone offer her that most liturgically British salutation, "Such fun, isn't it?" Winifred would offer a distant, distracted smile and say, "Possibly."

Having grown up in a small community, Winifred knew the value in not telling the natives how they ought to do things. But on occasion comments would drift from her mouth into the open air.

"I suppose the tea isn't too warm, so people won't be encouraged to loiter among the headstones and be reminded of how short all of this nonsense is."

Winifred Birkeland had respect for the ones who could claim that there had always been Starkadders at Cold Comfort Farm. They weren't so keen to fight people over a holiday shepherd's hut's colours not being in keeping with the scenery. They reserved their commentary for figures who made a great noise about the preservation of the countryside while driving their expensive cars across fields that weren't theirs, or those who let their precious untrained dog Balfour frighten flocks of sheep.

At the Ladies Society of Poldark meeting, Winifred would listen to well-known lifestyle figure Amanda Hampden (who would say upon being introduced to anyone, "Technically it is The Honourable Amanda Hampden, but I never use it. So quaint.") complain about having her view ruined by people daring to use the public path. Winifred recalled how when Balfour had killed three chickens the response had been, "They should have been kept in a coop and not allowed to wander the garden. Balfour was just following his nature." Winifred, knowing that Amanda Hampden only took oat milk in her tea, would add full fat milk. Telling herself that the tea wasn't contaminated. Just a bit compromised. Much like the Honourable Lady's view on property.

Occasionally Winifred would turn over the idea of making an effort at the dance of outward impressions. Only so she could exclaim, "God, how I tried." But Winifred knew it would be like trying to make soufflé for a hill-walking expedition or picnic: something that should never be attempted because she would find herself reliably disappointed in herself and the outcome. She couldn't be blithe about soufflés or precious conventions anymore.

§

One Wednesday she had agreed to make scones for the Ladies Society of Poldark's monthly meeting. (Held every third Thursday of the month, as the chairwoman Pauline Goonharvern could get her cousin to come and sit on that day with Pauline's inherited elderly pet parrot, Sacheverell, who would pluck itself bald as it didn't like to be left alone. "Very anxious. He hasn't been right since Mother died in '87. The damn thing won't do the decent thing and pass on.") Winifred began by brewing a cup of Earl Grey tea; while it grew in strength, she sifted together plain flour and baking powder. She wondered what made it all too much for her.

Was it just one too many declarations of jubilant admiration over duck egg blue curtains and magnolia walls? Two colours that displayed a kind of excruciating neutrality that bordered on being Swiss in personality. Winifred noted that those who adored that combination of restraint appeared uncomfortable around striking colour, like it might steal their handbag or seduce their spouse. Those acolytes of subtle good taste were the same ones who declared themselves "a bit naughty" when they agreed to a thin slice of cake that happened to have icing. That phrase would always make Winifred eat two slices of cake and add two sugars to her tea, even if it made her uncomfortably full and ruined her supper. It was quicker than painting her kitchen lime green.

Confusing to her was that the affected moderation was abandoned when it came to the manic interest in decorating objects. It was after having attended her second class with the Ladies Society of Poldark on decoupage that she began to understand why those in the Arts and Crafts movement were so keen to reject the cluttered novelty of Victorians. What next? Taking up shell craft to hold their opium in pretty boxes? Winifred had been gifted a small dish that had been marked like a sinner with the stencilled phrase, "Keep calm and carry keys." She slipped it into the village jumble sale just to see if it might disappear for the good of society. It was purchased by the sister of the woman who had given her that dish. From then on, she knew to take such things directly to the recycling centre. The man who worked there asked if there was something wrong with a clock that had been hand-painted with poppies and a Union Jack (a prize from a raffle). She told him that it had been cursed like a changeling. He nodded as if this were a common experience in his line of work.

Maybe it was the off-hand bigotry that made the tea taste so bitter. At the last summer village picnic, Mrs Wriothesley (with her third glass of Chablis) spoke of having to leave the city because she was tired of trying to learn how to pronounce the names of students. "I am not racist but most of these names just weren't British." And then a few others began to chime in about the oddness of names. Winifred found that she wasn't so hungry for a slice of Mrs Wriothesley's lemon drizzle. She wasn't going to put up with that dry cake and its grainy shellac of misleading satisfaction. She did offer to get the offending lady another drink and proceeded to water it down with some vinegar and water. Winifred felt that someone with such bad taste wouldn't notice anyway.

Winifred began to cut butter into the flour and blend it along with sugar until the mixture was like sandy crumbs. Would these scones be right? Winifred considered the years of trying to win in the baking category at the annual village show. It always went to Jennifer Jane Henderson. This year it was Jennifer Jane's cheese scones with saffron and dried cranberries that won. "So original," said the judges. Winifred's cheese straws with ras el hanout and Gouda were deemed "quite the experiment". Jennifer Jane came over afterwards with a scone and trophy and said, "Those must be very different. Curry isn't for everyone, is it?" Winifred smiled and said, "Good thing I didn't put any in it." She massaged a few extra seconds out of the awkward silence that had followed her words, because she was enjoying the fact that Jennifer Jane had lipstick on her teeth and Winifred had decided not to mention it. She merely said, "Well done you with those scones. Imaginative."

In the kitchen she realized she had forgotten to soak the sultanas in the Earl Grey tea. Winifred didn't really want to add them to the scones. She didn't want the tea either. She wanted these scones to stand on their own and make people remember eating them. But first she had to add most of the milk, and an egg, to the mixture. (Her Gran always told her to leave a bit behind: "You don't make things sloppy if you want success.") It was all coming together—like her possible plan for the meeting. She knew exactly how they were to be. As she rolled the dough out onto a floured surface and cut out scalloped rounds, placing them on a greased baking sheet, she knew this time there would be no interference or adulteration except at her hands. This brought Winifred to the one thing she had not forgiven: the honey cake (as it was known to her closest friends).

❧

Winifred once spent a morning making a chocolate hazelnut cake that did not need a great deal of adornment. Like a woman who had faith in a favourite scarf or tuxedo jacket—who didn't feel the need to have layers of perfectly colour-coordinated accessories to hide the doubt/discomfort of a chosen dress that didn't quite work—this cake had enough personality and flavour. The crumb was moist and didn't disintegrate when touched by a fork. When one sliced into the cake, a marbled delight was revealed. Winifred had pride in the cake. It was donated to the cake stall that was raising funds to improve the signage along the coastal path that implored people not to go to great lengths to get the perfect photo. The air ambulance was getting tired of rescuing people in elaborate dress from the rocks. The final straw for one rescuer had been the woman dressed as a mermaid who had thrown a fit when they left behind her coral statement necklace. She had screamed at him, "I was going to use it for a giveaway. Do you know how much revenue that will cost me?" The man found himself longing for winter storms, when stupid people chase after their dogs onto the cliffs.

Winifred brought her elegant cake to the village hall and placed it alongside the Victoria sponge, Bakewell tart, fairy cakes, brownies, and a suspect beetroot cake. Barbara Duffey was always guilty of trying to make cakes healthier. (She went through a phase when she swore that Brussels sprouts made a wonderful substitute in courgette cake.) The only ones enjoying her cakes were local pigs and chickens. Winifred knew Barbara was a kind soul who was eager to use things in her vast garden but felt she should have stuck to ratatouille or *sabzi khordan*.

Winifred had gone off and then returned to see what had sold. She noticed her cake was only a third gone and thought something looked odd. She looked at it more closely and noticed it was sitting in a pool of something sticky. Someone had drizzled a great deal of goo all over her cake and now it was soaking in a waste of perfectly good honey. Why had someone done this to the cake?

It wasn't a dry cake. It was a fairly sweet cake that didn't need to be made into a cloying disappointment. A friend came over and said, "I saw that. That did not seem like the sort of choice you would make."

Winifred said, "Someone doesn't understand cake. Or maybe they lack taste."

Winifred felt the irritation pullulate within her. That someone would think to know better than her about a cake of her making. She looked about for the organiser of the cake stall and found Gwendolyn Palafox holding a neatly folded tea towel and doing her very best at being a convivial, head girl sort. Winifred gently glided into the conversation, asking how much had been raised, what the crowds had been like, and how the weather had helped. She gazed out at the scene and then asked, "Gwendolyn, I am curious, did something happen to my cake? Was the honey used to fix a mistake someone accidentally made?"

Gwendolyn was a woman who liked immediate familiarity (the sort to say "rezzie" for reservation) but, like many of her set, did not enjoy confrontation—direct or indirect. She began to flit about in her bird-like way, refolding the tea towel over and over whilst building layers of weak excuses. "Oh, darling Freddie [no one called Winifred that except her sister], I felt it needed something."

Winifred asked, "Did you taste it before you poured on all of the honey?"

"No girly, I don't touch cake. New diet, no sugar except a spoonful of maple syrup once a week. But doesn't it look gorge with that extra touch?"

Winifred felt herself grow very still and she could not stop staring directly at Gwendolyn as she said, "It has a look. It must be difficult to know how it tastes when the honey touches everything."

Gwendolyn kept smiling but her eyes were looking for a way out while she repeated her declaration that the cake was lovely and wasn't the day just utterly fab.

Winifred finally said, "I wish you luck in selling the rest of the cake. I do hope we make a nice sum for the charity."

The rest of the cake went to the pub landlord's chickens. When there was another cake stall for the repair of the holy well, Winifred found herself away and unable to make something. She didn't want to risk a cake being terrorised with agave syrup or sprinklings of currants. Winifred did not want people to think she would do that to her cakes.

$$\clubsuit$$

Winifred brushed the leftover milk and egg mixture onto each of the scones and put them in the oven. Just one more touch, so that the ladies would not forget these on this occasion. Once cooled and split, she placed jam and cream on each one and put them on a plate she'd picked up at a charity shop that would suit the day.

The meeting included a short talk on the work of a local artist who created pictures of the sea using litter she found on the beaches. A decision was made regarding whether to take packed lunches or go to a pub for lunch on an upcoming day out to an estate with a garden that had an area devoted to poisons. (Winifred was sad not to be going on that trip. She was very curious about what might lie in that garden.)

And then there was tea and refreshments. Winifred offered scones to two ladies and one commented, "Oh, I see you have done it the Devon way." And the other said, "What is wrong with that? My Nan came from Honiton. She always did it like that." Winifred left them bickering. Then she offered them to some other ladies, and one said, "I see the Cornish have gotten you." Winifred kept moving about the room, creating discord but never offering her opinion.

The plate, once empty, showed an illustration of Cornwall and Devon. As they were bordered there were always comments about whether cream or jam should go first on scones in a cream tea. She wondered if anyone had ever thought to just turn them over if they preferred it one way. She knew that they enjoyed the ire. She wanted to give them this one last gift. She watched as several arguments developed. Some were now branching into opinions about the nature of people in Devon, and how someone's aunt had cheated someone on the price of some land. Winifred smiled and slipped out the back door.

A few days later Pauline went to Winifred's home to return the Devon/Cornwall plate. She found a sign outside the cottage that said, "To Let". No one answered her knock. Like the seeds of wildflowers, Winifred Birkeland was off to spread more of her lesser pandemonium.

ℰ

REVOLUTIONARY PLUM TART. QUICK.

Time is short. You know they are on their way. You have burned incriminating evidence. NO ONE will be taken and you know not to speak. You have trained for this. As for that other thing, they will never be able to figure out the code, and the instruments are hidden all over the house. There is a bit of time. You notice the plums are quite ripe and you aren't going to eat them. You aren't some poet, and there are so many of them. The plums, that is. Though there are many poets too. Most don't get into the kind of trouble you get into.

Slice up about six of those plums and put them into a bowl and mix them together with about three tablespoons of brown sugar and one teaspoon of cardamom and one teaspoon of cinnamon. Maybe you have some pumpkin spice and you choose to use that. If someone makes a wry comment about pumpkin spice, you will remind them later that you may use pumpkin spice but *you* didn't fink on the cell and give away secrets to the enemy. Better to be basic than a collaborator. Let everything sit for about 10 minutes. Use that time to write some letters to your loved ones. Tell one the secret to your rice pudding, another of a safe deposit box in an obscure bank in Zurich that will sort private matters.

Turn on the oven (390°F/200°C) and get a sheet of puff pastry and roll it out. Dock it except for an inch around the edge. This may be the last thing others will eat that came from you, and you want it to be lovely. Remove the sliced plums and lay them out in several rows (making sure to keep that one-inch border around the edge). Then brush a simple egg wash on the border. Bake for 18–20 minutes. You will use this time to pack and sew a few jewels into the lining of your clothes. This may be useful later. You hear the cars screeching to a halt outside; it is done. Remove the tart from the oven and it will cool. Now to keep your own cool. They are coming up the stairs.

❦

POET'S KISS, FROZEN

The memory of a kiss can be a shadow. We can see the shape of the emotion from the moment and might recall a scent. We chase it like children wanting to step on it and claim we possess it as the memory stretches at the end of a day. Did you make me want to keep pressing my lips to yours even when I was out of breath? Did I dream you kissed me as I was lying in your bed while the early midsummer light pushed through the windows, wanting to greet us against our will?

We tried to leave marks that lasted a little longer. The small bruises on either end of my clavicle that seemed to be borne from an urgent hunger where you were not going to take just one polite small serving. You were going to feast as much as you wished. I pressed those tender spots for days to try and bring myself back to that point when I could feel your lips holding tight as you tasted my skin and I was fed this frenzied recipe of rapture and pain.

You created a few more permanent marks with poetry. I read or listened to those over and over. Trying to pick them apart for a little more flesh to savour and hold onto for another day. I would never turn them down, for they sustain me in different ways. Often they make me laugh, which brings a warmth that is much like having your arm around me in that shy way of yours. Other times I think you write poems to steal my breath away so that you may hold onto it, until I am forced to retrieve it by offering you my lips and any other part that you crave.

While I wait until I can watch your face break into that open laughter, or we encourage one another with an amiable insistence to finish the last bite, or lure each other down odd streets, I will work my own magic, like Chione, and freeze pieces of ourselves, carrying your kisses within me and on my lips.

A conjuring of this kind begins in a simple way, with a potion of spices steeped in milk. The cardamom and vanilla bean are like the stories and opinions we have traded: strong. Never harsh on the tongue, but never uncertain. The milk has speckles everywhere, just like the ones you discovered upon my body with elation. With it comes a sweetness, which is like your sanguine nature. It makes me so curious at times, trying to understand where it comes from. I lean in to take in a bit more.

Once the pods have given up every part of their scent and flavour, they must be strained out. A custard will be created. Sugar and eggs together, tempered with the hot spiced milk, slowly combined. More opinions and feelings thicken this base. (We could each tell each other five different ways to eat eggs and why they are superior, appreciating with affection a good argument over the preparation of an omelette. Eggs do that to people.) Cherries are added. Perfect as they are on their own without adornment, I will always want to add them. I offered you cherries once before. Just one or two, you said. Then more. Those cherries were out of time and place, and they were better than they should have been. Those blushing cherries came to us different ways, and we probably know them better than some. In this custard they belong. Trust me.

Now to freeze our poet's kiss. The spiced cherry custard has to be removed from the heat, but it won't lose its constant arousing energy. The kind where we gently tease each other back and forth as if we are playing squash or badminton. You don't pay attention to the score, but you do want to keep the volley of silly clever comments going back and forth for as long as possible. You sometimes even let someone have a "win" because they make you smile so much. (Usually if they tell you a joke with a terrible wonderful pun.)

This custard is poured into a bowl with cold cream that sits over a bowl of ice water. We whisk and watch as it comes together, and there develops a tiny tint of pink. A trace of a bold shade worn by both one night. Then orange blossom water. Then, as it churns and this kiss becomes permanent, a generous handful of chopped-up pistachios. Some might choose almonds to go with cherries, but the flecks of the buttery green texture are better because we want just a little bit more of everything. We could have one drink, but we want at least two—especially if they are beautiful to look at. We could just have a short walk, but we want to see all of the city. We could just listen to that one song, but we want to talk about which is the best on the album, and then give each other songs as if they were small gifts left on each other's desks. We could just have one more kiss goodbye, but we know we need to kiss the whole four minutes before the taxi arrives.

Our frosted sweet kisses and memories are kept hidden away in a box to be carefully rationed out. This won't be for any old ice cream social. Maybe I am too greedy about your kisses. I will hold this poet's kiss on my tongue, and it will slowly melt, as I did in that book shop over your words about Auden. This shall be my ambrosia until you can kiss each spot on my body, while I intertwine my legs with yours and we become intoxicated over each other's eyes and lips again and again.

IMPATIENT COMFORT:
A CAKE RECIPE

You do not want a beautifully constructed torte that is a feat of engineering and alchemy of baking. You do not want a carefully aged fruit cake that was fed for ages and anticipated like the next messiah. You do not want the latest trend in baked goods that requires some peculiar mould, five kinds of sprinkles, and a flame thrower. You just want some cake, and you want it now, and you really don't want to go to the grocery store because it is eleven o'clock at night and you can't be bothered to wear real clothes. We are going to help you get that cake.

Get out one bowl, and one 8"x8" baking pan. You know what you usually use for brownies or, say, macaroni and cheese? That tried-and-true piece of Pyrex that has lasted longer than some relationships or governments? Grease and flour that pan. No parchment needed. If you are feeling like you want to make a tiny bit of effort and use that one heart-shaped pan you own and have maybe used twice, you can use that. But this is about using what is in front of you.

In that bowl you put one and a half cups of flour. Just your basic flour. (We are not going to make you look for amaranth or spelt.) Then you will add one cup of granulated sugar, one teaspoon of baking soda, a quarter of a teaspoon of salt, and three tablespoons of cocoa. Do you have the fancy stuff? Do you have the cheap stuff? I don't care. Neither should you. This cake is forgiving. It just wants to make you happy. Whisk those dry ingredients together. Add one tablespoon of vinegar, one teaspoon of vanilla, or whisky, or rum, or nothing. We are not sending people on quests in the night for delicious things. The delicious things are right in front of us.

Pour in half a cup of oil. (Olive, canola, rapeseed? You know what you have.) And then finally one cup of water. Straight from the tap of your choice. Mix all of that. Make sure the streaks of white disappear and things look pleasing and cake-batter-like. Yes, this recipe is vegan too. Because sometimes vegan people want cake at 11pm and don't want complicated substitutes. They just want some cake right then and there. Pour the batter into your cake pan. Bake it at 350°F/180°C for around 25 minutes. Sometimes ovens run hot and you can pull it out quick. While you wait for your cake, consider your beverage options. Maybe take a bath. Find a comfortable dressing-gown to wear and put on some slippers. We have to be ready.

Once the cake passes the toothpick test you can remove it and let it cool for about 10 minutes. Maybe 15. Does this cake need frosting? No. No, it does not; this is a cake that is genuinely low maintenance. It is the Dude of cake. Maybe if you are up for letting the cake cool for a while you can sift some icing sugar on it (because we all like a bit of excitement and the risk of aspirating on some icing sugar is a low-key way to do things). Otherwise, you can eat it as is. Maybe add ice cream or whipped cream if that is your way to do things.

You can eat this cake with just about any beverage. Tea, coffee, cocoa, wine, milk, water, the sweat of Idris Elba. It wants to work with what you have on hand. You will have a slice and feel cosy. You can lie on the sofa, ignoring the crumbs on your chest, and know that you have cake and you hardly broke a sweat. It is the cake of the present.

AMOUR DE POULET ON RYE

The day my love had her thesis defence, I roasted a chicken in her honour. I filled the cavity with lemon slices, and sprigs of rosemary. (To remind us of that one month we spent together in Greece and our hopes to return.) There was so much butter massaged into and slipped under the skin. She loved crispy skin the most. She would tell me every single time, "Chrissy, this is my second favourite thing to taste. You are my first." It was going to be a wonderful night celebrating the end of all her rigorous research and writing.

She had other plans. She said she had to let me go so that she could follow her next path. She didn't touch the skin.

I am home again in this city that I hadn't planned on returning to—we hadn't planned on returning to. Our plans were tossed into the trash like that awful roast chicken. I spend my days lost in the rhythm of gliding mustard across rye, placing onions on top of piles of salami, and slicing thick sandwiches—sometimes adding a pickle (always on the side, you don't want it to make things soggy)—for people who want to eat quick during their too-short lunch hour. My co-workers are the usual nomadic fun figures that populate the food service industry. They spend a lot of time talking about what they hope to do next. While you wait for your Havarti and ham, they wait to hear back on that audition, acceptance into a program, or that opportunity to go work in that exotic location. I am not waiting for her, or anything.

After the first rush, I was chatting to one of our regulars, Harry Chen. (His name is one word among everyone who works here.) He was seated at the counter for his weekly tuna sandwich. ("No onions please. They ruin everything.") Ever since he was widowed, he usually hangs about after lunch. While I was tidying up, we chatted about the hopes and inevitable disappointment that comes with following the Mariners. Harry Chen was waxing poetic about the perfect game that Felix Hernandez once pitched, when a man and woman came to the counter. The woman exuded that rare kind of sincere interest in everyone she encountered; she leaned forward and asked, "Hi! How are you today? Is the salmon sandwich good?" The man interrupted before I could answer. "She wants to know, what is the most intensely satisfying sandwich you have available today?"

She playfully yanked on the cuff of his shirt, throwing him a look of feigned exasperation that melted into obvious amusement. She asked him, "Are you going to be like this all day? It was bad enough on the walk over here." He told her, "You said you were incredibly hungry after that meeting. I am just trying to be helpful."

I let them finish their banter before I attempted to jump in. I said to her, "If you want something filling, I suggest the meatloaf sandwich. Everyone say it is a meal and a half."

The man said to me, "That is what the lady will have. Can I have the Reuben on rye?"

They paid for their sandwiches and went off to continue their mutual teasing in the small alcove seating. The Reuben was handed off to my co-worker Flora, who was sharing the morning's gossip from the adorable produce guys at Frank's with Javier the meat delivery guy. (She had plenty of time to chat while it was being toasted, and Javier wanted to hear the latest stories about people in the market.) I focused on the creation of the thick and deceptively moist sandwich that does not require many condiments to prop it up. (Some customers don't believe me when I warn them not to overwhelm it with ketchup.) Once the man and woman were served, I went back to organizing my work area. Harry Chen leaned across the counter and said in a low voice, "Hey, Chrissy."

"Yeah?"

"I don't think they're married to each other."

"Who?"

"That couple in the corner over there."

"How can you tell?"

"They paid separately. In cash."

"And?"

"They both have wedding rings, but they seem awfully familiar with each other."

"Harry Chen, you are looking for trouble."

"Just calling it like I see it. Being a detective for twenty years should count for something."

I watched them for a few minutes. They were having the best time talking to one another. He brought her extra napkins. She almost touched the corner of his mouth to point out where mustard had lingered. She encouraged him a couple of times to try her sandwich before he submitted. The bite itself wasn't such an intimate act; it was the way his fingers lingered over hers and stroked the hand that offered him the sandwich—not letting go until she took the sandwich away.

"Excuse me, but what is in your chicken salad sandwich?"

"Chrissy, you got a customer."

I was pulled from watching this cosy scene by Harry Chen's voice. I looked over to see a lovely Korean woman who looked utterly put together. Even her scarf was draped in a manner that defied the physics most mortals have to adhere to. She smiled when she saw that I had not heard her. It wasn't an impatient smile you often get from customers. Hers was genuine. She seemed delighted to be there. I quickly apologized and said, "It's your basic chicken salad. Dressing, chicken of course, and celery. Though today we are offering a special since we are low on mayo. It has a pesto dressing."

Her smile dropped a bit and said, "A bit of the 90s, eh?"

171

I laughed and said, "Something like that. It's quiet now; if you like I could make one with the usual dressing."

She perched herself neatly on the stool and said, "That sounds fantastic."

She tossed many questions at me. "Do you chop up the celery fine? What about the chicken? All white meat or some thigh meat? I like thigh meat because it is much more tender."

Harry Chen said, "You sound like a bit of a connoisseur."

She said, "I am always on the lookout for the right chicken salad sandwich." Harry Chen chatted to her and got the five-minute version of her life. (He always said, "Everyone wants to tell their story. Postman on the street, suspect in the chair, they all have something interesting to say.") I listened to pieces of answers about West Seattle high school, a brother, and a sister, and a few years in San Francisco, and gathered things. I mixed the chopped up dark and white chicken meat, the minced celery (the size of the celery depended upon who was making it. I have never liked finding thick pieces of celery in my food). And the dressing.

I looked up at her face, which just looked so relaxed, and asked, "What kind of bread?"

"White please. I like your scarf. You look really cute." Our lunch counter's one loose attempt at uniformity are the headscarves we wear to keep our hair out of the way.

I said, "Thanks. This orange one is my second choice. I wanted the pink, but Tim the Cook usually steals it. He says it is a power colour so he should get dibs, as he is the master of meatloaf."

"Let Tim the Cook have his pink. I think that your braids look so pretty with the orange next to it."

She looked so happy when I presented her the sandwich (I had added a pickle spear as a treat). She looked right at me and said, "I can't wait to try this, thank you."

"My pleasure."

Her gaze made me feel puzzled, my eyes darted about and finally concentrated on her scarf. I said, "I really like your scarf. How do you make it stay like that?"

After she finished her first bite she leaned in again and said in a dramatic stage whisper, "It's a knock off! The real version would cost my grocery bill."

As she ate the sandwich, she revealed to me that her co-worker Amaal had showed her a few tricks using pins in discreet places to make any scarf stay in place. Harry Chen began to draw her out about her work in the department store. I ignored the dishes for a few minutes and watched her be animated about everything. Every so often her eyes would meet mine as if we had an established intimate joke between us. At the end of the meal she said, "Thank you. That was nearly perfect. Do you ever use tarragon in the dressing?"

Tarragon. It reminded me of one place I worked a number of years back. They always insisted upon tarragon there.

I said, "Not really, but listen ... come in on Thursdays or Fridays just after the rush. I can concoct something for you."

"Would you? You are a star."

As she paid the bill, she handed me her card and said, "I am Megan Seung. If you ever need a discount on fancy scarves, come see me. Except on Mondays, which I always have off."

The mysterious meatloaf couple followed her out the door. Megan waved at me as she passed by one of the windows.

Thinking about that little wave distracted me while I wiped down the tables and counter.

Harry Chen said, "You should stop by and say hi to her."

"She's just a nice customer."

"Doesn't hurt to see what she is all about."

"I think that is called stalking."

"Is it all apps with you kids? When I met my wife and found out where she worked, I stopped by and said hi."

"Do you need a hobby?"

He stood up and grabbed his paper and said, "I am too busy. I exercise in the park, I have gambling on Tuesdays, and I pick up the grandkids from school. She's pretty. Don't be a dumb girl."

As he passed by the window, he gave me a mocking wave.

I had Tim the Cook order tarragon.

❧

Megan took to coming by every Friday. It was her treat to herself when she got paid, as she had to be responsible the rest of the week with lunch from home. She told me how Harry Chen had stopped by her work and bought something for his daughter. He had also taken her co-worker Carol to coffee. Megan said, "Chrissy, you should have seen how smooth he was. Whenever he stops by, he has all the women flirting with him."

"Yeah, that is Harry Chen."

"You haven't stopped by yet. We have some scarves that would look gorgeous on you. I think you should wear green."

"I will. Though I don't think most of what you have would be great for work."

"You should still come by. I wouldn't mind seeing you."

Why did she have to say things like that?

Harry Chen was right; she was absolutely pretty. She was also sweet, and kind. She always said thank you twice when I made her a sandwich. Once before she ate it, and again when she finished. She would ask details about the sandwich each week.

One Friday as Megan began to ask me about the ratio of mayo to sour cream, the mysterious meatloaf couple returned. I glanced over at Harry Chen, who appeared to be in deep conversation with Big John—one of our homeless regulars. Harry Chen would buy Big John lunch (grilled ham & cheese) and they would have their monthly memorial chat about the fate of the Sonics, and what they could have been.

This time the man ordered the meatloaf sandwich. The woman chose the turkey with cream cheese and house-made cranberry sauce. Again they paid separately and in cash, and sat in the corner alcove. When their sandwiches arrived, the man took a bite of his, and then handed it to her. He looked at her with enigmatic amusement as she began to eat her half of the meatloaf sandwich with such neatness. She had no problem holding his gaze. Was I witnessing some kind of silent dare between two people?

Megan began to examine her sandwich and said, "When I was a kid, my mom and aunties liked to go this one place up north for lunch. The restaurant did a turkey salad sandwich with the cranberry sauce on the side. It was canned but good. The turkey salad did have pineapple chunks, which was a little unusual. My Auntie Shirley thought it was a very elegant touch. I wonder if they still make it."

I asked her, "You seem to recall sandwiches with such detail. Are you trying to get me to recreate a certain sandwich?"

She tipped her head to one side and rested it on her hand, looking almost dream-like for a moment. She said, "Remember how I asked you about tarragon? There used to be a place on Third, I don't know if you know it, but they put tarragon in their chicken salad. I loved it, then they closed. I found another one quite a bit like it over on Seventh. A bit of tarragon, the celery wasn't too thick. They weren't stingy with the meat, and the dressing held it all together so well. I just remembered—the lettuce added a little extra crunch. Then that sandwich disappeared. The place remained, but no more sandwich. It's silly, but I do love the way you make me a sandwich each week and listen to all of my questions about it."

I knew the exact places she spoke of, but I didn't say anything beyond, "It's my pleasure."

After she said her second thank you, she grabbed her handbag and said, "Don't forget to stop by soon. Do I need to have Harry Chen bully you into coming by?"

"I will try. Really."

She said goodbye, and then waved at me again as she passed by the windows.

Harry Chen came over with empty plates and said, "Well, then. How long are you going to act like this?"

I ignored his question and took the plates away.

❧

The mysterious meatloaf couple passed by on their way out, telling me thanks for lunch. As they left, the man put his hand on the small of the woman's back, and said to her, "So smart of you to suggest we schedule meetings at the same time so we could come here."

Harry Chen said, "I should have bet you money. I would have cleaned up."

Harry Chen and Big John left to check out the book stall. I stood to one side as my co-workers chatted to each other. Tim the Cook suggested I take my break. I sat on a bench with my coffee and thought about the place on Third that I worked at during college, and the place on Seventh I ended up at while I waited to hear on my grad school applications. My then-girlfriend got accepted into her PhD program, so some dreams were deferred, but it had not felt like a sacrifice. Do I say, "That lettuce and bit of marjoram you probably tasted was my ex-girlfriend's idea. Glad you liked it."?

I asked Tim the Cook to order some canned cranberry sauce.

❧

On Friday the mysterious meatloaf couple appeared right after the lunch rush. They both ordered meatloaf sandwiches. They were almost giddy—maybe with hunger. If Harry Chen had witnessed the scene, he would have wisecracked, "Yeah, for each other." They raced to their preferred spot. Once seated they gave the impression of civility above the table, but I could see that their feet and lower legs were intertwined. They had the frenzied urgency lovers express when they are unable to access the sweetest parts they crave. I hoped their sandwiches would keep them from bursting into flames for a few minutes.

Megan appeared like clockwork with her perfect scarf, her gorgeous face and easy manner. I said, "Hey you, I have a surprise for you today!"

She sat down in her usual spot and asked, "What is it? Do I have to close my eyes?"

"Only if you want to. But it might be a few minutes."

I made her sandwich. Not the chicken salad sandwich she once knew, or the one we served, but the sandwich that I created for her. More dark meat than white meat (including the oysters of the bird—which are for the truly deserving), minced celery, mayo, sour cream, a bit of tarragon, marjoram, paprika, chives, with lettuce, on caraway rye, and canned cranberry sauce on the side.

I presented it to her and said, "From me to you."

She looked at everything and said, "Oh, Chrissy, thank you so much."

I found excuses to avoid talking to her while she ate. I grabbed anyone's dishes or utensils and rushed them to the dishwasher; I offered to grab supplies for co-workers. I had to find that imaginary bit of courage. She saved me from myself by asking, "Where is Harry Chen this week?"

Oh, thank god. I could handle that subject. I told her, "He's on his annual trip to Vegas with some old cop buddies. They go gambling and then go to this one dive that serves dumplings. He refuses to tell me the name of the place. He always says it is too pure and holy of a place to be sullied by a bunch of hipsters."

"Ah. Carol was asking after him."

"Her and many other women."

I began to go and look for something else to tidy when Megan stopped me and said, "Chrissy, can you stop going everywhere for a minute. I love that you made this sandwich for me."

I was waiting for anything to pull me away from this moment. Maybe the meatloaf couple would finally lose their minds and begin making love in the corner. Maybe Big John would show up wanting to talk about Shawn Kemp. Unfortunately and fortunately I had no way out. I said to her, "I wanted it to be just for you."

She touched her scarf, playing with the hem, and said, "I think you may have made the perfect sandwich. I also really like you."

Even though Harry Chen wasn't there to push me, I found more of my courage, because my soul felt like it was on fire. I was lost to her. I asked, "What time do you get off work? I am done at four and I can come and see you. If you are free afterwards, would you like to go somewhere? You could even come to my place and I could cook something."

Megan smiled and said, "I am done at five. I thought I was going to have to have Harry Chen pass you a note telling you that I liked you. Make me dinner. I am sure it will be fantastic."

Sometimes you can save the chicken and make something nice out of the wreckage. But I think tonight I will make her pasta instead.

℃

SHOWGIRL ICEBOX COOKIES

It has been some year, hasn't it? We always say that. But maybe it has been a bit too much year for you. Maybe in good ways. Maybe in challenging ways. Maybe it was a pile of failure cakes with too much sad syrup, and you have had your fill. Then comes a moment of potential good cheer with the holidays. For some there is that period of Advent, where many get that surge of energy and decide to make everything bright and beautiful and tempt the world with gorgeous offerings. You always say yes to what they hand out, because many of these things only come out at that particular time, and once again you fall in love with the scent of citrus and nutmeg and lingering pine. You want to reciprocate all that goodwill, but there are hurdles. Maybe you lack all the ingredients (because not everyone keeps great quantities of macadamia nuts in the house). Or you lack the physical and emotional energy to make five hundred different kinds of cookies and cakes. Which is okay. Not everyone has a full set of spoons to unleash on all the baked goods. You want to be a little bit extra, but you must ration it out.

There is a solution! It is a cookie that allows you to stretch out small amounts of luxury. Bowls will need to be gotten out. Just a couple. In one, you will whisk together 230 grams of flour, one teaspoon of cinnamon, half a teaspoon of baking powder, and a pinch of salt. It is patient. Then, in the other bowl, you will cream together 170 grams of softened butter and 200 grams of sugar. This cookie is going to look like Joan Collins all dolled up at the end. Then you add one egg and the zest of one orange. (You can peel and eat the orange later and tell yourself you did a good job and ate some fruit today AND made this cookie dough. You are riding high on accomplishments.)

Doesn't that smell lovely? Now you will slowly add in the dry mixture in three parts. Add some, mix everything together and so on. Success. Then you will add in 30 grams of chopped pistachios (because you only have a few left over from the time you were feeling lush and bought some for another baking project that never happened so instead you slowly ate most of them. Which is fine. They are good for you and you need to eat). Then you add in 45 grams of chopped hazelnuts. Two fancy kinds of nuts and not a lot of them. Because this cookie is a little show-off.

Then you mix in 30 grams of dried cranberries and 40 grams of dried cherries. Yes, Virginia, there is going to be colour and sophisticated flavour. In Britain there is a real love of dried fruit in assorted holiday desserts, but it tends to be heavy on the raisins and currants, which can be nice, but not everyone looks upon those with glee. Some think, "Oh great, you are ruining things with raisins. Again." You can bring this cookie around and say, "This is for people who need something that is a bit sexier."

But back to the big bowl (we are getting ahead of ourselves). Begin to gather up the dough and press it together. You will form it into a log. About an inch or so in diameter will do. This might be a bit fiddly and sticky. Here is a great truth about the creation of glamour: it requires labour, and it is often messy. No one shows up with perfectly-placed false lashes their first night out. There is art in the armour and drag set before us.

Now for the fun part: you will wrap the log up in cling film and put it into the fridge for a couple of hours. Or maybe the freezer for a week or two. You can take a break. You have done the first major step and that counts. Go take a nap. Go on with the rest of your daily life. Go watch that television series you are really into and makes you feel okay about things. Maybe you need to recuperate. This cookie can wait. (And if it doesn't get made until January that is fine. People can enjoy the surprise of cookies then. They might need it when the winter doldrums aren't showing any sign of lifting.)

Now a bit later you want to come back to it. Preheat your oven to 360°F/180°C and then brush a slightly beaten egg all over the cookie log. Then? We are going for full-on glamour with this cookie. You will roll it in sugar crystals. Red! Green! Maybe a mix of both. You choose something fun. Just make sure it is coated in shimmering goodness. Like a legendary burlesque show.

Now cut the log into quarter-inch slices. Take a moment to admire that cookie. There is colour! Two kinds of fruit! Two kinds of nut! Shimmer! It is a Vegas floor show doing two gigs nightly for the price of one. Lay those showgirls out on lined baking sheets. Bake them for about 15 minutes until the edges are slightly golden. Then let them cool. Showgirl Ice Box cookies are full of pizzazz that looks easy but is born out of a lot of hard work. Everyone who will glance at them and taste them will be in awe of their star quality. You can have another nap now.

APOCRYPHAL POTATOES
AND OTHER FAMILY LEGENDS

At Easter I made scalloped potatoes to have with dinner. Growing up, that is what we always had with Easter dinner if we weren't eating Chinese takeaway (a family tradition born out of my father's working on the holiday because he was a cook, a loose plan to go and have dinner at the restaurant he worked in, the car breaking down, and my mother deciding that she was DONE with the day and wanted some sweet and sour prawns instead). As I was putting together the recipe I realized how inexact it was. I learned to make it by watching my mother; occasionally she would make comments. "Don't bother peeling the potatoes. Just slice them thin and drop them in the ice water." "I don't know ... enough cream to cover them." "Yeah, they look done ... Who the HELL left a banana-peel behind the curtains?" It was a recipe that worked. When a friend asked how to make them, again it was inexact. "I dunno, enough potatoes to feed people."

What I could tell you about the recipe was that it had been in the family a number of years, and no one turned down a helping. (Except my children, but I have come to accept that their taste in things makes little sense. They are lovely people, but they think soup is too wet and grilled cheese sandwiches are gross.) I asked my mother more about the recipe. Here follows the interview.

Me: What is the complete story behind the recipe? I remember you saying an auntie or cousin got it from a place she worked at. It has always seemed like an elastic recipe.

Mom: Grandma[1] had a bunch of sisters [this is the "way back in the beginning" version]: Zelma, Alma, Helma, Melba, and Mabel. (As kids, we loved reciting the names. We thought it was hilarious that there was one that didn't rhyme. We were easily amused. It was before video games.) Zelma was my grandma—not necessarily a warm fuzzy grandma, but I absolutely knew she loved me. She is still the person I want when I am sick. Alma was her sister, a woman with dyed red hair and a real talent for picking the wrong man. I never met Helma or Mabel. But Melba I think was also kind of wild. I have the feeling she was kind of a good-time girl in her youth.[2] She was still bubbly and outgoing as an old lady.

Mom: Anyway. Melba had at some time worked at the Camelback Inn[3] in Arizona, probably in the 30s or 40s. The Camelback Inn was opened in 1936 and catered to rich folks and such. It was quite the zippy place. The fact that Melba had worked there was regarded in the family as an asset to our social standing. Hey, we were working class, what can I say?[4] And that is where she got the recipe.

---

[1] *This was her maternal Grandma (also known as Grandma T). My mom said she was often baby-sat by Grandma T and on Friday nights they would have popcorn and watch* The Flintstones *while my grandparents were out partying.*

[2] *EVERY woman in the family was a good time girl of one kind or another in her youth. Just saying. (Don't @ me, Mom. You know I am right.)*

[3] *Now known as the JW Marriott Scottsdale Camelback Inn Resort and Spa.*

[4] *Grandma T and her sisters were daughters of Swedish immigrants who were farmers around the Iowa/Minnesota border. My mom once told me that Grandma T didn't learn to speak English until she was seven when she started going to school. So to be a maid where Hollywood royalty hung out was something else.*

Me: I realized when explaining the recipe that I wasn't entirely sure how exact it was. I just remember that you slice potatoes really thin, let them sit in ice water, drain them, put in a dish (I butter the dish just so it is easier to get things out) with many layers, maybe add a bit of salt half-way through because I am like that, and then cover in cream. Add salt and pepper and then bake at around 375°F (because my oven is like that) until golden and bubbly and the potatoes are tender. Am I missing anything?

Mom: So the basic recipe is as you described, except for one particular. No salt, no pepper. Just the potatoes, sliced thin, soaked in ice water. Put 'em in the dish, pour whipping cream over the whole thing, and bake it. Knowing my family, it was probably 350, even 325, because damn but that wood stove gets hot enough in the summertime[5]. Bake it for maybe an hour. I remember asking my mother about the salt and pepper, and she said no. Just potatoes and heavy cream. I think there was some kind of superstition that salt and pepper would somehow affect the mojo. Or something.

---

[5] *Grandma T had to keep a stove going year-round in Minnesota from morning to night. Every single recipe she ever shared kept the oven at 325°F.*

RECIPE FOR DISASTER
(HOW TO MAKE SMUG MUFFINS)

To begin with, you will preheat the oven to 375°F/190°C. Look for a muffin pan in the cupboard. I am not smug enough to have it in a special place where it is beautifully held. My muffin pans live in a narrow cupboard that holds cookie sheets, madeleine pans and baking racks. I dig about in there wondering if I might run into Mr Tumnus (no fur coats, though). Grease the muffin tins. You lose smug points if you have a non-stick pan as those are now to be feared. I think it causes your children to read V.C. Andrews or something—I don't recall the exact study. You can grease with butter or olive oil. You can gain a few extra smug points if you choose something like grape seed oil or an obscure nut oil. I prefer butter, as I am Scandinavian and I believe it is good for my soul.

Now to mix your ingredients.

In a large bowl (hopefully something ceramic or hand-made by a woman who offers wisdom in haiku form to well-to-do women interested in eco-tourism) you will combine one and a half cups of whole wheat flour, half a cup of oats and a quarter cup of ground flax seeds. Flax seed is the cornerstone of your smugness. If you can somehow replace the whole wheat flour with some semolina or another vaguely twee flour, you will feel the sort or pride reserved for mothers who mention, in an off-handed fashion, that little Cardenio and Nell don't like to eat French fries and that they ask for extra helpings of beet crudité with breakfast.

Returning to our recipe, you add a third of a cup of firmly packed brown sugar. OH NO, SUGAR!! It's okay. It's organic. (At least you tell people that.) You can still toss your hair in a superior way. Throw in half a teaspoon of baking powder and three-quarters of a teaspoon of baking soda. Add one or two teaspoons of cinnamon and a quarter teaspoon of salt. Now you are probably wondering, how can I up my smug factor with salt or baking powder? Well, make sure the salt is from an exotic location. The baking powder? Use something that is free of aluminium. Mix your dry ingredients nicely together and oh life is grand because you care so much about your family that you make these muffins for them.

Now to add the wet ingredients. One and a quarter cups of milk (you can use soy/almond milk if you wish), one egg (the egg should come from a hen that you personally know and with whom you occasionally have tea) and a third of a cup of olive oil. You can replace the egg with applesauce if you don't do eggs (a quarter cup of applesauce should work). Make sure you make the applesauce yourself and that you know the orchards where the apples come from. (You should have an intimate relationship with the orchard. Does it have a sordid history? Are there family secrets?) Remember, when people eat your muffins, you want to be able to give them the life story of each ingredient. Otherwise, you won't win at the end of the day. Finally, you can add a banana if you aren't a locavore. Another option is dried fruit or some other seasonal fruit. You want to be able to say while eating your muffin and sipping your green tea, "Yes, this is satisfying. I feel sad for people who have to survive on shop-bought muffins."

Give everything a quick mix. You don't want to over-stir the batter. Scoop/spoon the batter into the muffin cups. It should make twelve. Bake them for about 18–20 minutes. They should rise nicely and be golden.

When no one is around you can smear the muffins with butter and Nutella and eat them with the kind of desperation people in Europe must have had after years of rationing. Then lie around with crumbs all over yourself while you watch your favourite reality show and read that new tell-all memoir with the insert of glossy pictures of long ago. I won't judge you.

ℰ

JERUSALEM

"These are like a pea under a mattress. I would feel them if I was a princess."

"Aren't you a princess?"

"I was a countess, but I would still feel them."

Mimi grabbed one of the little knobby bastards, as Letu called them, and began to try to peel another. She disliked how quickly the topinambours (Jerusalem artichokes) dulled her knives. For Mimi this meant more frequent visits to the butcher who sharpened her knives. A man who complained about everything except the presence of the Germans, as he was making money from them. Mimi disliked how she needed him for more than a chop or a fillet. (Not that those were in great supply anymore.) Aurélie once asked her mama why she continued giving this man her custom, and Mimi explained that he was loose with talk of his own importance and sometimes he accidentally gave away good secrets. "He is a useful fool. He thinks I flirt with him and gives me extra bones."

The Germans had taken Paris. They treated the city like a selfish man who enjoys humiliating his beautiful lover in public. Then the greedy bores decided they also wanted the potatoes. In exchange they gave everyone rules with dire consequences, and topinambours. (Jerusalem artichokes to everyone else.) Just like the occupiers, the little tubers seemed to invade the rest of their life. No matter how the artichokes were cooked, they gave everyone wind. Letu tried slicing them very thin and adding them to a salad. Her husband Yves said, "My darling Ledu, this was very interesting, but please do not make it ever again." His stomach made so many noises in distress that his patients were concerned he didn't know how to take care of himself. Aurélie entertained everyone one Friday night with her tale of a German soldier trying to flirt with her on the metro, and how she couldn't help but fart in his presence. She said, "Auntie Sora, the artichoke and leek soup you fed me for lunch saved me from having to go out to the cinema or a bar. Please keep some handy for when I must go out on my own." Their friend Eztebe had foraged for mushrooms and tried sauteing those with the topinambours to put them on toast. His wife Pilar said it needed jamón. Pilar usually said that about most dishes. Eztebe said, "It tasted of very little, yet it smelled so much later on."

One night there was a debate as to whether they were being punished, or if the tubers were part of a secret cell to overtake the Germans. Mimi thought that the Jerusalem artichoke had to be communist, for they lacked style but had a habit of going on and on, like they were giving a bad speech. Yves felt differently. He said, "It is very ugly. It does turn on you quickly like Pétain. It must be a nationalist. I don't think the artichokes are Catholic royalists as they are not covered in jewellery and lace." This image so amused Sora's companion Klara that she began to sketch the Jerusalem artichokes as little characters. She made one look like a well-fed Cardinal and gave it the caption, "It is the scent of holiness you are experiencing. Almost like roses, no?" Yves insisted upon giving Klara several cigarettes for the sketch. She did not smoke, but Yves knew they would keep them in bits of offal for Berthe the dog. Letu later told Mimi that Yves had framed it and put it in the water closet.

Mimi didn't like how they did so little and still took up space. In less charitable moments she said they were the sort of thing that Mirosław would have unloaded on her. Mimi found, as she tried to listen to the illegal radio, that they made far too much noise when she was peeling and slicing them. She muttered to the Jerusalem artichoke she was peeling, "Your conversation is as diverting as a rich man talking about his car." They trusted most people in the building, but she hesitated in turning the knob up on the radio. Upstairs was just Letu's family, and the man in the hat who remained vague about his origins but was helpful to all. The squabbling couple across the hall had disappeared to Normandy at the start of the occupation with the agreement that Mimi would check on things, keep the fern alive, and dust once a week, as the half-deaf concierge Madame Bazin below them was a bit of a snoop.

Everyone knew Madame Bazin was loyal in many ways, but she liked to be fed cognac and gossip—and if either was in short supply, she went looking for it. Gossip lasted longer and was easier to obtain. She preferred the petty stuff—who had a feud over a clothesline, who always had a lot more cheese than their ration permitted, and whose wives flirted too much with the fishmonger who had ten children and a tired wife. She had little interest in the occupiers or their desire for information, as she was still angry over their people taking Alsace in 1871. She was born five years after it had happened, but the event had broken her father's heart, and she inherited his grudge and tended to it like a shrine. Madame Bazin had enough visitors that Mimi knew to keep the radio quiet.

Though today she turned it up a bit, as they were playing music. It was Molto vivace from Beethoven's 9th Symphony. Mimi liked this movement a lot—especially after Klara told her that Beethoven wrote it to sound faster than it was, and that the movement wasn't in the usual place for a symphony. The music gave her hope that there might be more than one rebellious German who created beautiful things.

Mimi and Letu quietly raced against the music to finish the vegetable prep. The two middle-aged women usually had much to say to each other as old friends, but there was pleasure in working together in silence, as there were so many sounds outside that brought anxiety. These days Letu was quieter when she was waiting for her son Enzo to return from one of his mysterious trips on his bicycle. To keep her and his papa safe he would only say he was off to visit friends in the country or he was going fruit picking. Often, he would come home with something delicious that was difficult to find in most shops. Once it was a large basket of raspberries. Another time it was asparagus. (He had traded his rubber boots for them.) Everyone had gathered one afternoon and eaten them cold with a vinaigrette. There was mutual agreement in the post-gastronomic glow that Spring had never felt so fine. Other times Enzo would bring back mysterious packages, or people, but even curious Letu knew to embrace a useful ignorance and only ask, "Shall we keep them downstairs across from Mimi or upstairs in the attic?"

Mimi didn't feel it was necessary to fill the air with false reassuring words. They just needed to focus on finding dominion over these lousy root vegetables.

When the movement had ended, Mimi nodded towards the radio. Letu turned it off and put it away in its present hiding place, an English bread box. The metal box was a curiosity picked up by Pilar and Eztebe in a flea market. Pilar thought it was so pretty with the hand painted flowers on the door. They had both felt that the bright yellow box would make the perfect Christmas gift for Mimi's warm kitchen. It had spent much of its life with Mimi holding gloves, keys, spare matches, and whatever else didn't have a proper home. Now it held secrets.

Mimi wiped her hands off and removed her apron. The gingham fabric was made up of the remains of a dress once made for Aurélie. The pink fabric was faded and stained; it made her recall those days when no one had any money, but potatoes and butter were easy to find, and everyone said yes to another glass of wine while someone was playing violin or guitar. Letu brought her back to the present, "What shall we make tonight? Soup again? Boulangère? I might have a few lardons in my kitchen." Mimi massaged her hands that felt the cold much more than they used to. She paced about the kitchen tidying, neatening the insignificant things, as she considered what dinner might be.

Amal had brought her the Jerusalem artichokes when he came home to hers for lunch and his nap. Mimi still wouldn't allow him to move in, but they had found a pleasing compromise that he spent his lunches in her kitchen, and in her bed—except on Wednesdays. Mimi knew it was the day he went and gambled with friends from the market. He insisted she needed a day to lunch with her friends and he shouldn't be too selfish with her time. (He always appeared in the evening with small gifts from any winnings, and she would make him a real cup of coffee, the only treat she could offer once a week.) As they were lying in bed, she thanked him for the artichokes. He pulled her close onto his chest and said, "My sweet lady, one day I will bring you potatoes, as I can't promise you palaces or gems."

She caressed his chest and told him "I have already had those. A potato would make my heart sing."

"Yes, instead of your ass."

Even on the darkest days, Amal could still make her bark with laughter.

She promised him it wouldn't be soup again.

❧

"Letu, let's make something different. Is Yves going to be here tonight or will he be at the hospital?"

"Hospital, but he is hoping to come home before midnight."

"Keep the lardons another day. Maybe a gratin if we can find a little cheese? I have a little milk."

"I do have garlic."

They began to make a list of what little there was in each of their homes. One had some greens. The other had vinegar. Well, it wasn't really vinegar, it was some wine that wasn't very good. Any oil? Just a little bit and it was a bit old. But one couldn't complain. There were some walnuts in a cupboard. And there was one tomato on the plate. It looked so lonely that it needed to be eaten up. If they made it to the bakery, they should be able to get a bit more bread to go with dinner. They didn't eat together every night, but when there wasn't much in the cupboard, it made everything less bleak when they could fill in the gaps on the plate, and they could save a little bit of fuel.

A knock at the door interrupted their careful plans to defeat the limitations of the market. They did their well-practiced check around the room that nothing was out of place before Mimi answered the door. It was Enzo! Mimi called out to Letu, who came rushing in to give her son a hug.

"Have you eaten?" These were always her first words to him.

"Never enough." This was always his response to his mother.

He followed the two women into the kitchen with his rucksack. He accepted a small glass of wine and the last of the morning's bread. The two women stood expectantly, wishing they could offer him more, and hoping he would hurry with his words so they might get to the bakery. He said, "Auntie Mimi, a present has been offered for the help you gave in keeping some precious things safe before they could be sent home."

Mimi said, "I always have room. Remember the lamp I had for three years because my cousin Felix kept putting off picking it up? Of course, he decided to take it with him when he ran off to the south of France. Your mama wondered if he had money hidden in that lamp. Your goods never overstay their welcome."

The most recent "goods" consisted of a heavy suitcase that sat on top of her wardrobe. It belonged to a woman who spent a few days in the apartment across the hall until she and the suitcase could be spirited away by Enzo and one of his friends.

Enzo pulled out a great wheel of reblochon. He had been quite far on his bicycle. This cheese came from Savoy. Both Letu and Mimi wanted to ask where he had been to get such a prize. He said to them, "Your efforts have been appreciated and someone wished to thank you." Mimi was thrilled to have something so filling. Letu threw up her hands to snatch the idea thrown to her and shouted, "Tartiflette!"

Mimi smiled and said, "Of course! When was the last time we had that? We took the train so many years ago."

"When Enzo and Aurélie were children."

"That was wonderful, wasn't it? And the wine."

"We don't have potatoes."

"Maybe the topinambours will do. With enough cheese?"

They wanted to share this cheese with everyone. Enzo was told to try and find bread, and if possible, something sweet for dessert. And that he must see Amal and tell him to bring his mother Fatima to dinner for a surprise. Letu went upstairs and telephoned Klara and told her the household must come to dinner. (They never said Sora's name, as she was surviving on false papers.) Klara said they would bring some cherry brandy they had hidden away, and they would bring their ancient dog Berthe, who had to be carried up and down the stairs like a queen (yet still had the appetite of a puppy). Then Letu telephoned Aurélie at the clinic and told her to tell Yves not to stay late, as there was something decent for dinner.

She returned downstairs with an onion, decent wine, and lettuce. There was to be a feast tonight. The great pan was brought out onto the old range. Onions were cooked down until they nearly melted, the lardons were sauteed, and the Jerusalem artichokes were sliced like little coins and partially cooked. Enzo returned home with some bread that Letu described as barely decent, and a few pears. He also said that Amal would arrive as soon as possible. Enzo would have been home sooner, but he had to say hello to Madame Bazin when she saw him in the courtyard. He said he gave her a pear and told her he heard the fishmonger was to become a father—again. "She appreciated both gifts and told me to stop by for a slice of bread and jam tomorrow—like I was still a boy."

❧

A dish was prepared—with layers of potatoes, the onions and lardons, a little wine, a little cream—and the reblochon was sliced in half and arranged rind side up. It wasn't quite like it was with potatoes, but they thought it would do. Mimi and Letu kept smelling their fingers after touching the cheese, as it was so very different from the ersatz scent of life under occupation. Nothing smelled bright and clear anymore. So many things smelled grubby or tired. The cheese was aggressive and hadn't fallen to the Germans.

As the tartiflette cooked in the oven, Letu prepared things for a salad. Mimi laid places at the large table in the other room. Klara and Sora arrived first. Berthe insisted upon lying on the old settee like a dowager duchess who would claim she was near death's door even as she attended the funerals of everyone else. Klara and Sora were like her ladies in waiting as they surrounded her and petted her and spoke of her troubles. "Up half of the night." "She doesn't like it when the soldiers appear on her walk." "Poor dear Berthe," murmured Enzo sarcastically to the aunties as he opened the wine. Letu smacked him on the head and told him to offer them a drink.

Amal and his little mother Fatima appeared. She removed from her handbag a little bag of almonds and proudly offered them to Mimi. They had been sent from her daughter Sofia, who remained in Marseille with her husband the artist. Fatima also shared news of the south and paid her respects to Berthe, who sniffed excitedly at a fellow little old lady.

Mimi removed the tartiflette from the oven, but it didn't look quite right. She called in Letu, "Maybe my memory is off, but it appears a little too soupy."

"Let it cool. It should be fine in a bit. The cheese looks as it should."

They decided to let time improve it as they waited for the last of family to arrive. Yves and Aurélie walked in looking exhausted. Aurélie wandered off to her bedroom to remove her coat, shoes, and elements of the day. Yves waved at everyone, touched Enzo's head, and kissed Letu. He asked, "What is the magic you have conjured tonight?"

She fixed his tie and said, "Enzo brought us something from the past."

Everyone sat down at the table to eat the salad and enjoy the wine. Then Mimi brought out the tartiflette. There were a few gasps of delight, but no questions as to how it happened.

Yves looked at it closely and said, "What recipe did you use?"

"The usual one."

"It looks different from what I recall. It isn't creamy."

"Letu said it should be fine."

Mimi shared it out. There was the usual silence in those first bites. But then the silence felt odd.

Something wasn't right. Mimi said, "I think I used the wrong wine ... Or maybe the cream curdled. This isn't good."

Yves asked, "Which potatoes did you use? These taste off."

"We didn't. It was the topinambours as usual."

Sora added, "Oh, thank goodness; I thought I had lost my sense of taste."

It was Fatima who said, "No starch. They don't have any starch, so it falls apart."

Mimi muttered, "The little bastards." She threw her napkin behind her. The topinambours had completely ruined a potentially wonderful dish. Mimi was so upset trying to figure out where she went wrong. She had wanted one lovely dish for everyone after so many months of deprivation.

Amal poured her another glass of wine and said, "You can blame me. I owe you so many potatoes."

Letu told her, "The cheese is still good. Let's eat the cheese."

Everyone picked out the bits of onion and the lardon or two on their plate and everyone at the table reassured her that the cheese was wonderful. No one had anything that good in such a long time. Yves pointed out that scraping the cheese onto the bread improved things. The rest of it though? A lost cause.

They knew they couldn't afford to waste anything, but it was just too awful to eat. It was suggested that maybe Berthe might like the remains of that terrible dinner. When the dish was placed upon the floor, she leapt off the sofa and proceeded to eat every last bit of the failed dish. She pranced happily around the table asking for petting as she wanted to show what a useful dog she was.

Then Berthe proceeded to vomit her dinner all over the kitchen floor. Sora was mortified, but Mimi laughed and said, "She was a gracious guest, as she did it on the kitchen tiles and not upon the carpet. Berthe gave me the most honest opinion about dinner."

Everything tidied, Enzo took Berthe for a short walk, in case she needed to expel any more of the wretched dinner. Dinner wasn't going to defeat anyone. Everyone sat down again to slices of pears, the almonds, and small sips of the cherry brandy. Mimi placed the radio in the middle of the table like it was a cake. She turned it on. They leaned in as they held their glasses. *"Ici Londres! Les Français parlent aux Français ... "*

𑀘

WHAT A DEAL

No service on her phone. Still.

"Anything for you?"

"Nothing. Even that damn cat game isn't working."

"Then everything is well and truly over."

The crisis had come so fast. People had gone into work that morning reading the news that talks had fallen through, again. This was expected. Usually, they would resume after a few days of dramatic sulking by either side. But then his Excellency began to make declarations via his favourite medium. By lunch, threats were being made from either side like a divorcing couple who suddenly decided that they each had to have that ugly wardrobe out of spite. Work meetings were interrupted with calls to come and watch what was happening on the screens. Everything was collapsing. The checkpoints were closing again. People made calls to family, getting plans in place.

"If I don't make it home tonight, I will make it home before Thursday. Yes, I remembered my pass … I love you too."

"It might be too dangerous on the roads tonight. You know how the guards are. Would you mind feeding my cat?"

"Let me talk to the kids. No … Just say I went to see Grandma and will be home before lunch tomorrow."

He had missed the last train, as had she. They sat together on the bench as people milled around them trying to find ways home before the central checkpoints shut for the night. Otherwise, it meant staying put. They didn't join the crowd that had found a bus taking people east. He kept trying to pick up a signal.

He said, "Maybe if we wait until most go away there might be enough of a signal to get through."

"Of course. Maybe you could climb onto the roof."

"Oh, don't be silly. In these shoes?"

"I always find it difficult to picture a man like you, wearing shoes like those. You are almost ... dare I say ... a hipster." She smiled in reference to the mock insult he had once lobbed at her on their train rides home.

"Heartless. The world is ending and you choose to make fun of my shoes?"

"Just trying to keep a few things normal."

"I think normal burned itself to the ground before teatime."

"I wonder if we went elsewhere, you might be able to get a hold of your spouse to let her know you are safe."

"All of the phone lines are down. Are you hoping to find a random farmer in the city with a ham radio?"

She gathered up her handbag and coat "It is a good thing you are charming, otherwise I would have kicked you in the shins a long time ago," she said, "You should come with me. We can go somewhere and wait."

"Where do you wish to lead me?"

"Normally I would say to your doom, but someone else has that covered."

He picked up his bag, "Where to then, lovely?"

"A pied-à-terre that belongs to my boss. I am the keeper of the spare key, as he is always losing his. I bet there are copies of that key across much of Europe. He might still have Wi-Fi or something. At the very least we will be warm, and he probably has a few bottles of something worth drinking."

"That sounds more civilized than huddling in the train station. Lead on."

As they made their way down the street away from the station, they saw plenty of people about. There wasn't the same full-on hysteria there had been when the last emergency happened, but everyone was trying to get somewhere, anywhere. A few spontaneous parties had erupted here and there. People were on stoops and in courtyards, offering others food and drink.

"Oh, come on ... forget your clean eating, just drink the goddamn wine, Nadine."
"I am going to eat this entire cake. I don't care anymore."
"I spent all that time on my skincare regime. And for what?"

They didn't say much to each other as they weaved in and out of the way of others going in the opposite direction. He followed her for several blocks before they turned to a side street. They slowed their pace and he began to walk beside her.

He said, "I haven't been anywhere that wasn't in public with you. I hope you won't rob me."

"I hope you won't murder me. I just thought of that as we were on our way. 'What if this guy rapes and murders me? That would really ruin my day.'"

"Oh ... of course. I promise to not rape and murder you."

"I will only rob you if you have a lot of money."

"I don't."

"I suppose we just have to have a nice evening together."

"I can put up with that."

She switched her bag to her other shoulder and poked about in it looking for her phone. She found it and saw it still lacked a signal and was quickly losing battery life. She said, "Before I left work, I read an article about the history of the Doomsday clock; and why it recently has been moved forward another thirty seconds."

"Has it?"

She dropped her phone back in the depths of her handbag and said, "This might be your big opportunity."

"Closer to doom is my opportunity? You sound like a terrible salesperson."

"For three easy payments, you too can enjoy the end!"

"That sounds like a bargain since I won't be around to make the other two payments. So what are you selling tonight, Miss?"

"Do you remember when we put each other on our lists of people we would sleep with if the world was going to be no more?"

As they waited at an intersection, he smiled. "We may have had a few drinks when this was discussed. I recall incredibly specific parameters to this deal."

"I have spent enough time with bureaucratic sorts to know that creating specific guidelines makes a great deal of sense. It leads to fewer instances of confusion or rejection by another party."

He looked at her and said in a sardonic tone, "Nothing sexier than a carefully organized fling."

She gave him a blithe shove. "Hey now, I think if such a thing comes to fruition," she said, "both parties should have a very good time. Also, I am incredibly fond of you, and want to be considerate."

"Even if the world is ending?"

"Especially if the world is ending."

Cars passed and they continued across the street. Lights were coming on, and they could hear sirens in the distance that alerted to the closing of most checkpoints. He touched her shoulder and said, "You are in my top two."

She looked up at him grinning and said, "Two? How did I make it up so high? Who am I competing with?"

"Just a television star. I tried phoning her, but she was a bit busy with five other people. It's not much of a competition."

"Just a television star," She parroted, "I hope you don't mind that I am at least fifteen years older than her, and likely to have experienced the ravages of gravity and time."

"As long as you don't mind a sad, old, greying man in his forties."

They started walking again.

She said, "It would be a pleasure. Unless you disappoint me. Damn. I should have asked for references."

He laughed and said, "See, that was your first mistake. For someone who claims to be organized and has everything sorted for a one-time liaison, you should have double-checked before putting me on your list."

"I am willing to take the risk."

"I think that one of the reasons you made it to the top two is that you are kind to me, though I can't really fathom why you are, given that I am just some man with whom you share a commute. I must confess, I think you are bewitching and rather attractive."

"Do you know why you made it onto my list?"

He shook his head.

She continued, "The first time you smiled at me, it left me thunderstruck. Your smile was just so charming that it gave me an honest-to-God headache. I couldn't quite decide whether I wanted to smack you, or leap upon you and demand that you make violent love to me. The only sensible thing for me to do was decide that if circumstances were ever in my favour, I was going to insist upon the latter—oh, we're nearly here," she said, pointing towards an apartment building.

He stood there for a moment looking rather pleased with himself before saying, "Oh. I wasn't even trying to be charming— well, that's not true. If I find a woman interesting I want to get her attention, but this feels a bit like dumb luck."

"It might be. Now would you mind holding my phone and wallet while I try and find the spare key in my bag?"

He said, "Not that I want to delay this adventure, but we could first have something to eat? I feel like my blood sugar is beginning to drop. I didn't have anything sweet this afternoon."

She adjusted a shoe that felt tight after a long day of wearing and too much walking. "I don't think there is anything in the apartment," she said, "but I know of a place around the corner. Also, I am hungry. I don't want to bite you too hard."

"I wouldn't mind that."

She took his hand, and asked, "Are you sure?"

It was a rare instance that he couldn't keep up with verbal volley. He resorted to a slight cough of surprise. She laughed and said, "Feeling all right?"

They walked a few more blocks before arriving at a taco joint that was open. It looked like a party was going on with people wearing hats, tossing balloons, and random objects at each other. The man in charge shouted over the music and people that they had to get rid of everything as the freezer had died, so everything was free. "As many tacos as you can eat. Just don't ask for mild salsa—we're out."

They did their best to follow that directive. They had many margaritas with quickly melting ice and told each other stories. He spoke of his dear wife, their kids, travels, why one kind of cookie was superior to the other. She mentioned a husband and children who were everything precious to her. She told embarrassing hilarious stories with tenderness about the girl she had once been. He gave a passionate defence of certain bands and acted out how he ended up with a scar on his ear, the result of trying to wrestle a tent whilst drunk at a festival in his youth. She knocked over a glass of water while explaining why a certain film was underrated, and tried to justify how stealing Christmas trees was a form of radical liberation. They were two fortunate souls, who were given the opportunity to give their own eulogies.

He looked down at his drink and said, "I wish I could get hold of them. I left a message while the phones were still up, but I said I would call again. What about you?"

"I spoke to them earlier. I know they are safe, and they know I am safe. He told me to stay here if I couldn't get home. Also, I refuse to let the world end tonight."

"I didn't realize you had that much power. I might have insisted upon a slightly more upscale location for dinner."

"My power is so great that anything else would be disappointing. Tacos are what we need at a time like this."

They ate tacos with too much cheese, meat, and salsa. They chose random things from the menu because they liked the way it sounded when they over-pronounced the Rs. They had churros even after acknowledging they were too full. The owner insisted, saying, "If you don't it will go to waste. You need a sweet or two." It was worth burning their lips on the deep-fried sugary pastry. The frenzied hurrah kept going on around them as they began to play with each other's fingers, whilst sipping the briny cocktails.

He told her, "Your face is quite pink."

"Yeah, well your tie and shirt are rather rumpled."

"I wasn't trying to insult you."

She waved her hand at him in a slow, but dramatic fashion, leaned forward, and said, "I know, I know. My face always gets like this after a few drinks. This didn't happen until I got into my thirties. Ugh. Is this what it means to get old?"

He leaned in and spoke in a close manner like a spy sharing his latest conspiracy, "You don't know the meaning of old. Look at me. I am a broken-down old bloke with bad knees and so-so cholesterol. A walking tragedy. You just look like you blush a lot which is rather funny."

She touched his face and snorted with laughter, before summoning up all her energy to sit upright to show all the drinks had not taken complete control over every muscle. She slapped the table and said, "Okay old man, let's go before I pass out in these tortilla chips."

He began to look for his bag and laid his hand against his chest before muttering, "I think I ate too much. Again."

She said, "We will walk home. That will do you good." She began to hiccup and added, "Oh bother. This is going to hurt so much later."

They said goodbye to the owner. Giving him hugs and telling him how truly wonderful he was. And wasn't this whole crisis an utter shame? It took another fifteen minutes before they were able to leave. The kitchen staff and several customers were hugged and told how exquisite they were as well.

He slipped his arm around her waist and said, "Lead the way home, scout."

She leaned against him and said, "Wouldn't it be funny if we came back and the apartment was full of people?"

They began to laugh and had to stop and sit on the curb for a few minutes to collect themselves. She helped him up and they held hands tightly like two young children, each squeezing each other's back and forth like a code. They whispered stray thoughts that appeared like soap bubbles in their inebriated heads. Sudden bursts of existence that seemed so solid popped, gone again to be replaced yet another. The streetlights were too dim. His Excellency had announced earlier that day that energy must be saved by everyone in this crisis. It made it difficult to find the spare keys in her bag; the battery on her phone was long gone. He held his phone over her handbag so she could find her key.

She said, "I really ought to thank you."

She stood on her tiptoes, found she was more unsteady than usual, grabbed his jacket for support, and kissed him. The kiss quickly turned from being a one-sided event, as they tasted the whispers of salt on each other's lips from the drinks they had had and felt the rising ebullience that threatened to overwhelm their ability to breathe.

It took several more kisses before she felt like she had thanked him enough (and he felt he had expressed welcome in offering such assistance) and was able to unlock the door. They raced upstairs to the apartment, which thankfully was up only one flight of stairs. When they reached the top, she caught her breath and said, "This place lacks an elevator. Imagine living on the fifth floor."

He leaned against the wall as she unlocked the door to the apartment, and said, "I have terrible knees from a running injury that has never truly healed. If the apartment had been up at the top we would have to do it right here."

They entered the apartment and she switched on the lights to reveal a living area that was rather stark and Scandinavian. White upon white, with imported wood floors made to look weathered, to give the impression that many generations had trod upon the planks. Beyond that initial shock of intentional simplicity there was odd decor that looked vaguely folksy, but also uncomfortable. Dried plants artfully arranged in vases, votive lights on a bracketed shelf made from reclaimed wood, a single wooden chair next to an ottoman that looked like a mutant sea urchin. A sofa that had no arms, and a short back, but did have a draped blanket that could be best described as institutional grey despite costing an obscene sum. In the centre of the room there was a space age coffee table, which was decorated with one single heavy art book about brutalist architecture. He looked about and said, "This looks cosy. Why all the sticks and candles? Is your boss a monk?"

"I think this was the influence of his last girlfriend. Dagmar, her name was, or was it Bente? I have no idea. They all look a bit like Claudia Schiffer, but more malnourished. Do you want a drink?"

He sat down on the sofa, trying to find a comfortable position, "Do you have anything for indigestion? I shouldn't have had that third carnita."

"Yes, why did you have that third one? That was ridiculous after all the other things we ate."

"It was free. It might be my last one."

She went to the bathroom and found some chalky tablets and something a ghastly pink colour that would have been more suited the aisles of toy shops filled with crazed-looking dolls. She brought them into the living room and held them up like prizes. She said, "I may take some too. I should know better than to eat all that cheese and then the churros. I am going to wake up in the morning and feel like death warmed over. "

"I shouldn't have eaten all those onions and chilies."

"We really are idiots."

"You are a pretty appealing idiot."

"You, sir, know how to get a girl out of her pants."

He held his hand out for the bottle, took it, and began to pour a shot of pink goo. He said, "Before we go any further can we wait a bit? I want to make sure this stuff works. Otherwise, I will be miserable."

"Of course. I should have some water. I hope it takes away the pink on my face. How about we watch something?"

"Is there a TV in this white box we call a living room?"

"There is behind a panel. My boss told me that Dagmar or Astrid thought televisions were uncouth and must be hidden so as not to ruin the spirit of the room."

"Is there anything on besides the speeches of the half-wit we call his Excellency?"

"I suppose not ... but wait a moment."

She looked through the carefully Kon-Maried set of drawers in the hall and found a few DVDs.

She brought them into the living room and pointed at one, "Have you seen this?"

He leaned forward and squinted. "I forgot my glasses at work. Is it any good?"

"Of course it is. What a silly question. It has Stephen Tobolowsky."

She put it on and they sat on the sofa to watch it.

"Are there any cushions or is that uncouth too? My back and everything."

"Let me grab some from the bedroom. I need one as well. I think these sofas are only for people who are twenty-three, do a lot of Pilates, and have excellent posture because they don't eat gluten, or something."

She returned to find him with his eyes closed.

"Don't fall asleep on me."

"I was just picturing you undressed."

"Of course."

Once the movie was on, she joined him on the sofa. Like a cat deciding they wanted a space, she put a leg over his, leaned against him, and began to play with the collar of his shirt. Like any person familiar with the habits of a cat (or an affectionate woman), he gracefully accepted the sudden positive attention, even if it meant he couldn't get up for a while.

She asked, "How many drinks did we have? I feel a little tired now that I am sitting down."

"You can't fall asleep. Only four. Maybe five. I definitely had six. I will keep you awake."

"You will? Oh, you are a pet."

He brushed her hair back and began to kiss her neck, eliciting a muffled giggle.

She said, "You may have to stop that."

Confused, he asked, "You don't like that? What do you like?"

"I do. A lot. But I am afraid that I might get hiccups again from laughing. And then I might be unwell."

"I will just have to touch other things instead."

"Fair enough."

"You don't sound terribly excited by that idea."

She smiled and said, "Touch away. I just feel a bit sleepy. Please. Do touch me. I like how warm you are. Like a rather sexy hot water bottle."

He burst out laughing at her attempted compliment, which she found catching. Once they had calmed down, they wrapped themselves around one another, engaged in an increasingly listless pawing of each other's bodies whilst commenting on the film. But sleep fell upon them before the credits rolled, and before they had the opportunity to make good on their plans.

The sun hit them in the face. There were no curtains or blinds, as the decorator girlfriend had left before the completion of the project.

She felt her face, which was puffy and tender. She muttered, "Oh dear God ... we are still here."

He squinted at the light, found his phone, and said, "We are. And my phone has a signal!"

She plugged in her phone and found she had one too.

There were messages from spouses. The news showed the talks had resumed. The crisis was over. They were given a bit longer to worry about everyday details, like paperwork and whether the bathroom needed repainting.

They replied to the messages saying they were safe.

He looked around for his shoes. "I want to go home and get into my pyjamas," he said. "I need to get some milk."

She massaged her hands, tinged with the beginnings of arthritis, and replied, "Me too. I need to do laundry. I am just going to call in sick."

They looked at each other and laughed. He looked like a man in his forties who spent the night passed out on a too-short sofa paying for it with back pain and pins and needles in his feet. She still had the remains of make-up from the day before. Her hips were bothering her from contorting herself into odd sleeping positions next to a tall man who snored.

She handed him his ridiculous shoes, and he made sure she had the spare key.

They left the apartment and went downstairs to the new day.

They walked to the station and took the train home. As they neared his stop, he got up and said, "Thank you for giving me a place to stay."

"Of course. I would do that for any friend."

"And next time—"

She tilted her head in surprise and said, "Next time?"

"Oh. I am sorry. I didn't mean—I shouldn't assume. I am a bit stupid."

"No. Next time, we will stick to light snacks and *then* have sex."

𝒞

A CHRISTMAS DINNER GUIDE FROM THE NATION'S MOST RESPECTED FOOD MAVEN

It is late Christmas Eve afternoon. Most of the presents are wrapped. (At least the ones you are in charge of are. They have been ready for a couple of weeks because you know better.) Everyone is in the living room listening to carols, sipping warm drinks, and helping the children with a puzzle.

You are in the kitchen, having a minor breakdown. There is dinner tonight to focus on, prep for Christmas lunch tomorrow, and somewhere amid all of that is midnight mass, present opening, breakfast, phone calls to relations further afield, and more games (games were invented by people who had servants and never did the laundry).

Someone calls out, "You should relax." These people are amateurs and should never be listened to, as they don't know how to correctly put the silverware in the dishwasher. But they might have a point. You can relax with this straightforward guide to Christmas dinner.

Christmas Eve
You already know what you are having for Christmas Eve dinner. Lure members of the family into the kitchen like they are audience members at a panto to participate in various bits of preparation. It makes them feel useful, and it gives you time

to freshen up your lipstick or drink as you give them directions. We enjoy a slightly rustic approach to Christmas Eve dinner. It is a slight nod to the holy family, who probably lacked ham and a passionfruit pavlova on that fateful night. There are drinks and an amuse-bouche or two to keep everyone entertained. (We don't say nibbles in this house, as nicknames are reserved for family members and enemies.)

While people chop things in their disorganised fashion (do tell them thank you and what a great help they are), you can assemble the stuffing. You can choose to stick with a traditional stuffing, or you can try something deeply historical or very modern. Be an agent of chaos at the holidays, and don't be too precise when bringing mayhem to everyone's expectations around the big day. Don't say, "I added a bit of cumin." Look at everyone and say, "It's interesting. You like interesting things." You do not have to be passive-aggressive, nor do you have to listen to the criticisms of people who can't find the right cream in the supermarket.

Stuffing should be a loving marriage between comforting and decadent. Plenty of bread and fat, and a few ingredients that tell the world that you know how to have a good time. Take any opportunity to add chestnuts, apricots, and good quality brandy. Now place that in the fridge and tend to the rest of the evening. If anyone says anything about how you should leave out milk instead of whisky for Father Christmas, tell them that Father Christmas has a much higher tolerance for alcohol and is lactose intolerant. Do be generous with the mince pies, as he has a very long night. He would also be grateful for a bit of cheese and crackers. (He can handle *some* dairy if he takes a pill or two.)

Christmas Morning

When to begin? When will you eat? To answer those questions we have to consider a few things. Do you have young children who get up like they are bakers? Do you have teens who wish to sleep in much of the morning? When do you open presents? Before or after breakfast? The correct answer is before breakfast. The children can eat the chocolate and sweets from their stockings, and the adults can live on tea and coffee along with any baked goods that have accumulated over the past few days. We must model passionate abandon to young people, and this is a fine way to do it.

Now you may be worried about that turkey or goose and when to put it on, along with the stuffing. Do not let the anxiety overtake you. I advise getting up while the children are enjoying the contents of their stocking. Go into the kitchen, remove the bird and stuffing from the fridge and let it come up to room temperature.

Then you should take a low dose of psychedelic mushrooms. You can have it ground up in a few capsules or in a tea. If anyone offers to help you say, "Do put more wood on the fire, and could you put on some music?" Sip that tea, turn on the oven so it can pre-heat, and then join everyone in front of the tree. I find these mushrooms take the edge off the big day. No anxiety and total focus, but you may find yourself colouring pictures with the children with great intensity, or petting the dog while whisper-singing Joni Mitchell songs. So remember to keep the timer on things.

If you are looking to eat around two, then try and get things into the oven about 8am. Remember you are not beholden to any particular time today. If you are cooking a turkey, make sure it is well-buttered and seasoned. Goose doesn't require any help with fat, but if the mushrooms have kicked in you may find yourself a little weirded out by its incredible wing-span and greasy skin. Do some slow intentional breathing and remind yourself it is merely poultry. Stuff the bird, and place in the oven at 390°F/200°C for 40 minutes. Then reduce the heat to 320°F/160°C. My preferred method with a bird is to drape some cheesecloth over the breast of the turkey. I ladle stock over it now and then. Not everyone has a taste for meditative tasks, and that is fine. You can always tent the bird with foil, but it won't be as interesting or flavourful.

You are now in a wonderful place. Take time to admire the tree and people's presents. The colours are utterly exquisite, and you fall in love with a bauble, for it captures a piece of your childhood.

Remember to open some presents and discover bliss. You don't feel the need to stare at the clock or become short with everyone for not recognising your labour. There should be talk about breakfast. Have everyone help to lay it out while you listen to the music and discover new depths to Ella Fitzgerald's voice. Let it wash over you. A continental style Christmas morning breakfast means no one has to stand over the stove and everyone can eat leisurely and happily.

It is good to get everyone involved in the process. Have the family peel and slice potatoes and place in water. Take this time to send a few Happy Christmas texts to friends and family. Send a flirty text to that one person you met at last month's party and now follow on social media. It is all in the spirit of good cheer.

Are you a bread sauce family? Now is a good time to make the milk portion of that sauce. It is wonderfully medieval isn't it? It almost makes you want to cook up some frumenty or serve a peacock. Once that is done, set it aside to keep on the warmer. Wander off to get dressed. Today is a good day to wear pretty things with the right amount of comfort. Right down to the knickers. Lace or something sheer is just the thing.

Once dressed, you can make the cranberry sauce. When the sugar and water are boiling, add the berries. They will burst apart with excitement. In your altered state you will be delighted how they come to life. Reduce the heat. You can give those berries a stir and then go into your larder or pantry and do a quick upskirt pic to send to your lover in another time zone so he can wake up to that enticing image. Remember, home-made gifts are often the most appreciated ones.

Once the cranberry sauce has set, remove from the heat and place in a beautiful dish and go and enjoy some more of the morning with everyone. Put out some biscuits, fruit, maybe some olives. Just a few light things to keep everyone happy. Don't be tempted to take more mushrooms. You are in a good place and anything more might have you trying to climb the Christmas tree like a cat. Sigh happily a few times. If anyone finds it odd just say, "I am in a wonderful place with the best people." Because you are.

Christmas Day Noontime

Have a look at the turkey, add a little more stock and consider removing that cheesecloth. It is now time to let it bare its breasts and brown up like you did last summer on that holiday in Corfu. (The tabloids did have fun with that.) Now par-boil those potatoes, drain them and give them a good shake. I like to hand this task off to another member of the family. They do love it and know to be generous with the goose fat and salt. I have no memory of how it happens, but they appear.

There should be other vegetables for Christmas dinner. There are a few ways to approach this. I prefer to cut up a bunch of Brussels sprouts, carrots, and parsnips, dress them in olive oil and herbs (sometimes I add a bit of maple syrup or treacle to create a caramel smoky touch to the roasting process), and pop them in the oven to roast. It may be the appropriate choice if you are in a slightly dizzy state with the mushrooms. Very little effort is required, and you can describe it as a rainbow mix of vegetables in a dish if anyone asks why it is all together.

It may be time to remove the turkey and let it rest while you make the gravy and those potatoes are allegedly roasting. While you are at it, pop those pigs in a blanket into the oven. Tell the older children it is their job to keep an eye on the timing for that, because you are staring out the window at the birds and wondering what it would be like to sing as part of a dawn chorus. Still, you don't feel a grand pressure to perform, because all of it will come together.

I find psychedelics in appropriate doses are a good choice for the holidays. You can be present and you aren't numb to the world like you might be with too much alcohol. And you aren't aggressive like you might be with some class A drugs. You want something that brings gentle calm and appreciation for the moment.

I should confess that I can be lazy with timing because I happen to have two ovens. I suggest having two ovens if you can. It is like having a few men in one's life: it keeps it interesting and tends to all of your complicated needs. Now we are getting close to dinner. Vegetables sorted, sauces and gravies thickening, potatoes nearly in place, and that turkey is ready for its moment in the spot-light. Make sure to have some drinks ready, and the table should look lovely. While you make sure that looks just so, take a quick shot of your cleavage and send that to someone special with the promise of something more with their Christmas cracker. All good things should be revealed slowly.

Now there may be questions about bread or Yorkshire pudding. I am of the mind that it should be simple and not a great fuss. I like having rolls warmed up, but I encourage you to find the right thing that makes you utterly happy.

Dinner is now here, and it is truly a gorgeous sight. Everything will taste exceptional and not just because your senses are heightened and you are kind of excited about that one photo that got sent to you just before the turkey was carved. You raise your glasses and embrace this beautiful day. If you do everything right, everyone will have a few moments of silence as they eat this grand feast.

It is now that you realise that you completely forgot about the Christmas pudding, but that is okay. Earlier in the month you bought a slightly fancy one from the upmarket supermarket and you can pop it in the microwave for a few minutes. No one will be the wiser, and you can quickly whip together a brandy sauce and open up the clotted cream. Add some lovely port with that and everyone will be satiated. Always keep a pudding about. You never know when it will be useful.

There will be games and dishes to wash—make everyone else participate in those activities while you go outside "for a bit of air" and hug trees like the pagan you are at heart—and eventually there will be naps. Follow this method and everyone will have a glorious day.

On Boxing Day you will still feel that residual calm and not be bothered by the let-down or anyone asking why there isn't enough of one kind of cheese. Just smile and say, "Shops open tomorrow. Have some brie." Then go off to sext with your lover for a little while as everyone watches the Doctor Who special on the television. Do avoid any dull curries for leftovers.

ℰ

ACKNOWLEDGEMENTS

As this is like an Oscar speech, I must be brief and emotional. Somehow I defied the odds and have been incredibly fortunate. Don't bother with an MFA. Just write a lot about everything, and have some life experiences that are very messy.

Yes, I wrote this whole book on my own but many people had a hand in me arriving at this point.

My first grade teacher Donna Proctor, who taught me how to read, and how to wrap a present (the two most useful skills of my life). She encouraged my story writing, and she introduced me to Beverly Cleary. A writer who made me want to write too.

All of the library workers in my childhood who worked at the Port Townsend Public Library. You kept me in so many books. You even gave me my first job, where I learned so much about people and their reading tastes. (Like the internet and fetishes, there is something for everyone at the library.)

Maggi O'Connell and Vivian O'Barski, who read a lot of early drafts. They are people who should be hired for their opinions on everything.

Jacob Meyer, who first hired me to write whatever I wanted to write, and who generally encourages all of my weirder ideas.

Clare Golding, who told me to call myself a writer when I balked at doing such a thing. Your energy and tenacity to get things done is something we need more of in the UK.

To the following people: Danica King, Kairu Yao, Kate VanDerAa, Rachel Thibodeaux, John Kelly, Abu Kasem, Kris Holt, Kai Mistry, Ann Scranton, the Blanchard-Wright family, Craig Church, Chris Hawley, Kurt Reeser, Rebbekka and Molly Riverstone, Angela DeManti, Kat Gwynn, Ben Hall, Margaret Houston, Sarah Emery, and my weird and passionate friends from Snarkfest. There are pieces of you in this book, and your presence and friendship means everything.

Bookshops enable and save people on a regular basis.

Spencer Thorn in Bude kept me sane during the harder days of various lockdowns.

David Hartman, who didn't live to see this day, but I think he would have been amused. Some of my happiest early memories are of sitting in his book shop Imprint Bookstore (in Port Townsend) and looking at picture books.

The wonderful people at The Second Shelf. It was there that I found a book that kept me going towards the end when all I really wanted to do was cry.

Angel Belsey decided a long time ago that I was going to write a book. I am glad that I decided not to be scared, and said yes. More people should listen to her, she has great ideas.

My agent Emily Sweet who has had the faith and patience of a saint that this would happen. I will always appreciate your wild belief.

My entire extended family is filled with storytellers, and I must give special attention to my siblings Tom, Kitty, and Michael. They are the funniest hard-working people, and they shaped my outlook on so much.

I got through this lonely, frustrating, and surprising process with my children Biscuit and Onion, and my husband Andrew (who never thought it was silly when I said I wanted to be a writer.) Thank you for your patience, and your easy-going manner while I got lost and tried to find my way out again.

Finally, I must thank my mother Theresa Chedoen, who taught me how to tell a story. She fed me so many fairy tales, and showed me how to get up every single day and make something.

ABOUT THE AUTHOR

When Genevieve Jenner was six years old, she liked to play dress up and write stories, and she wanted to be a mermaid. She has finally accepted that being a mermaid isn't the most secure career option, but the other two things have remained constant.

genevievejenner.medium.com
@gfrancie

Ƈ

ABOUT DEIXIS PRESS

Deixis Press is an independent publisher of fiction, usually with a darker edge. Our aim is to discover, commission, and curate works of literary art. Every book published by Deixis Press is hand-picked and adored from submission to release and beyond.

www.deixis.press

9 781838 498726